J. R. PICK
SOCIETY FOR THE PREVENTION
OF CRUELTY TO ANIMALS

MODERN CZECH CLASSICS

J. R. Pick
Society for the Prevention of Cruelty to Animals

A Humorous – Insofar as That Is Possible –
Novella from the Ghetto

Translated from the Czech by Alex Zucker
Afterword by Jáchym Topol

Karolinum Press

KAROLINUM PRESS, Ovocný trh 560/5, 116 36 Prague 1, Czech Republic
Karolinum Press is a publishing department of Charles University in Prague
www.karolinum.cz

Cover and graphic design by Zdeněk Ziegler
Typeset by DTP Karolinum
Printed in the Czech Republic by Těšínské papírny, s. r. o.
First English edition

ISBN 978-80-246-3699-3 (hb)
ISBN 978-80-246-3729-7 (ebk)

CONTENTS

CHAPTER 1

IN WHICH TONY TEACHES MR. BRISCH TO SING
AND GETS AN OUTSTANDING IDEA IN THE PROCESS

Tony, the hero of our story, was neither smart nor stupid. When the Germans came, in 1939, he was eight years old. He imagined he was in store for an incredible adventure—getting hold of a gun, say, and shooting one of Hitler's mustachioed aides-de-camp. Tony pictured all of Hitler's aides with mustaches like the Führer's, but looking at photos of them he was disappointed to see that none of Hitler's closest colleagues had a mustache, and no one ever gave him a gun either. Soon he was wearing a Star of David and attending a Jewish school. He wasn't much of a student. He tried to explain it away by pointing out that he had transferred from another school, but no one listened, since all the students had transferred from other schools, and they all tried to use it as an excuse. Eventually Tony became a messenger for the Jewish community, which only made him neglect his schoolwork even more. When he was eleven, he and his mother, Liza, left for the ghetto. Tony quite liked it there. Like everybody else, of course, he assumed one day the war would end and everything would be fine again. For Tony, *fine* meant he could go to the movies and eat hard-boiled eggs for supper at least two days a week.

Now, Tony lay on his back in the sick room in L 315, watching a fly on the ceiling. The fly was clearly bored. This was no surprise to Tony. He was bored too. Not that he minded being around old men. By now he was used to it. But these old men were boring. Mr. Abeles, for example. All he ever did was rummage around in his suitcase and moan and groan. Yet he had almost nothing to speak of in his suitcase and no reason to complain. He had a bed of his own, all he could eat, and spent his time in pleasurable company. Whereas the fly had no bed, finding food was a major chore (who in the ghetto would leave any leftovers?), and it was all alone. But you never heard *it* moaning and groaning like Mr. Abeles.

Tony grew to like the fly more and more with each passing day.

Imagine the fuss Mr. Abeles would have made if he had to crawl along the ceiling with his head hanging down! At the very least, he would have complained that he was going to fall or get stuck in a spider's web.

"Vatchink flies, eh, Tony?" said Mr. Hans Brisch from Berlin, Herman Göring Strasse 7. He used to play violin in a bar. "Zat cannot be a very interesstink occupation."

"Actually," said Tony, "this fly is pretty interesting. It reminds me of Mr. Abeles."

"Come now, Tony," said Mr. Glaser and Sons, "you shouldn't say such things. Whatever you may say about Mr. Abeles, he isn't a fly."

"What is that supposed to mean?" Mr. Abeles objected. "I'm a respectable businessman. Just ask anyone in Kolín: Abeles, on the square."

Mr. Abeles and Mr. Glaser and Sons bumped heads in similar fashion at least three times a day. All Mr. Abeles had to do was remark on how blue the sky was that day and Mr. Glaser and Sons would reply that thank God his eyes were still good and if Abeles couldn't see that cloud he'd better get his eyesight checked, and on it went from there.

At first, Tony found it funny. Sometimes he would even provoke the two men, asking Mr. Abeles, who had an alarm clock in his suitcase, what time it was, and Mr. Glaser and Sons, who didn't have one, whether it was correct. But eventually Tony realized that once they were finished shouting, it always ended up either with Mr. Abeles storming out of the room to the toilet, or the two of them angrily turning their backs on each other, and he felt sorry he'd ever started it.

So now Tony paid no attention to them, instead focusing on the fly. Then a new source of entertainment appeared on the horizon. Actually, not on the horizon but on Tony's leg. A flea bit him. Tony, being an experienced flea hunter, began to toy with it. Of course he could have caught it right away. But why not have a little fun with it first?

The men, noticing this, broke off their argument.

"Another flea, eh, Tony?" said Mr. Abeles grumpily. "No doubt that's because you're always washing yourself."

He was referring to the fact that Tony washed relatively often, and thoroughly. Most people think that fleas like filth. But they're mistaken. The truth is, fleas love a freshly washed body. Probably because it makes it easier for them to find their way around.

"I've got the little beast," said Tony, pinching the flea between his fingers and drowning it in a glass of water on the nightstand. The nightstand was the envy of every patient in the hospital. In L 315 there were only two: one in the doctors' room and the other one here, in room 26.

Apart from the glass for fleas, the table was also occupied by a thermometer, two books, and three toothbrushes: Tony's, Professor Steinbach's, and Mr. Löwy's.

Among the patients in room 26 there were also significant differences of opinion concerning the brushing of teeth. Mr. Abeles and Mr. Brisch believed it to be a needless extravagance.

Brushing your teeth, according to Mr. Brisch, damaged the enamel, and besides, you lost the bits of food stuck between your teeth. "I'm not so vell-fed zat I can afford to spit out my food," he would say.

For his part, Professor Steinbach thought brushing one's teeth was essential to good hygiene. Mr. Löwy took the compromise position: Brush your teeth, yes, but insofar as possible, don't spit out the bits of food.

"You must be pretty experienced," Professor Steinbach said to Tony. "I couldn't have caught it so quickly."

"I'm bored," said Tony. "Just sitting here catching fleas all day long."

"What else are you going to do," said Professor Steinbach, "with it raining all the time?"

It was always raining in the ghetto. And when it rains in the ghetto, it's bad. For one thing, you can't go outside or you might catch a cold and make yourself even sicker. For another, the potatoes get wet and rot. On the other hand, though, if all the potatoes were to rot, it wouldn't be so bad. At least then they could have dumplings.

Tony closed his eyes and imagined it raining dumplings: a whole mountain of them pouring down, so many they wouldn't even fit in the yard at Hannover Barracks that they used as the soccer field—puffy and white, and when you poked them with your finger,

the sweet, brown plum preserves inside would come oozing out.

Next, he imagined assembling two soccer teams from the men in L 315: Mr. Brisch, lying by the window, at left wing; Mr. Abeles, by the door, on the right. Tony, of course, would play center forward. Opposite him would be Professor Steinbach, with Mr. Löwy, by the door, at left wing, and Mr. Glaser and Sons, by the window, on the right. The men from the other rooms could play halfback and fullback—maybe the head doctor at center half, with Nurse Anna and the ex-nun Nurse Maria Louisa as defenders. The only position he left open was goalkeeper. With an all-star like Albie Feld in the ghetto, it seemed almost blasphemous to consider anyone else.

Tony's thoughts were interrupted as Mr. Löwy, who used to own a grocery store in the village of Dolní Počernice, told a joke with a double entendre, which Tony didn't get. None of the other men seemed too impressed either. Maybe it was Mr. Löwy's delivery. If Johann Sprengschuss, from the Freizeitgestalltung,[1] had told the same joke, they probably would have split their sides laughing. But then again, maybe not.

---

1) Administration for Free Time Activities, a Jewish-run organization, set up by the SS, which mainly promoted soccer and the arts.

"Goot joke," said Mr. Brisch. "Just not fery funny. But zat doesn't bozzer us, does it, Tony? Now vee are goink to sing."

Every day, from eleven o'clock to eleven thirty, Tony and Mr. Brisch sang Czech songs. It may have seemed more logical for Mr. Brisch, a former musician, to teach Tony to sing, but in fact it was Tony who taught Mr. Brisch. It wasn't just about singing, you see. For Mr. Brisch it was also a way to improve his Czech. Either way, the bottom line was that Tony knew the Czech songs and Mr. Brisch didn't.

"What have you got planned for us today, Tony?" Mr. Löwy inquired. He was the only one who listened to them. Professor Steinbach always stuffed his ears with cotton, and neither Mr. Glaser and Sons nor Mr. Abeles had much of an ear for music.

"'Broken-Down Oven,'" said Tony.

"I'm not sure this is the right time for that one," said Mr. Abeles. "Yesterday my cousin Magda Sauersteinová went with the transport, even though she had a serious case of sciatica."

"How about 'Fast Flows the Water,' 'Little White Dove,' or "Hey, Slavs,'" Mr. Löwy suggested. "Those are a little more serious."

But Tony still wanted to teach Mr. Brisch "Broken-Down Oven." For one thing, he had the feeling

Magda Sauersteinová wouldn't mind, and for another, he wasn't so sure Mr. Brisch could learn "Fast Flows the Water" or "Hey, Slavs." His Czech was pretty good, but dialects still gave him trouble.

In the end, Tony won out.

It's doubtful whether any musicologist would have approved of Mr. Brisch's singing. Doctors, too, would likely have objected to having a tuberculosis patient sing. But none of them could deny its beneficial effect on his mood.

Mr. Abeles, however, was outraged. Mr. Brisch sang out of tune, he said, and it didn't seem right for a German Jew from Berlin to be singing Czech songs.

"At least shut the window," he said.

"Open it vide," said Mr. Brisch. "It's a vonderful song."

"But what if it's forbidden?" said Mr. Abeles.

"Vhat forbid?" said Mr. Brisch. "Cherman songs zey could forbid. As members of an inferior race, vee cannot sing Cherman songs, but Czechish songs are all right. Ze Czechs are also an inferior race."

"Prove it," said Mr. Abeles.

"It is not me who says so, but Adolf Hitler," said Mr. Brisch.

"And naturally whatever Hitler says is sacred to you,"

said Mr. Glaser and Sons. "You ought to be ashamed of yourself."

Mr. Glaser and Sons didn't like Hitler or Mr. Brisch. There was nothing odd about that. He didn't like anyone.

But Mr. Brisch was no fan of Hitler either. "Hitler for me is not sacred, he is an agent of imperialism."

Mr. Brisch was a member of the Communist Party and made it clear whenever he could. Still, Tony liked him best of all the older men. Even if Tony didn't believe that Hitler was an agent—he made too much of a ruckus to be an agent, in his opinion—and the revolution seemed more distant to him than it did to Mr. Brisch—especially when, in a fit of magnanimity, he declared Mr. Abeles, Mr. Löwy, and Professor Steinbach to be members of the proletariat—he fully agreed that Mr. Glaser and Sons was a stuck-up capitalist and as such should be liquidated.

"Gentlemen, gentlemen," said Professor Steinbach. "There you go again, making a mountain out of a molehill. Why shouldn't Mr. Brisch be allowed to sing? Especially when he enjoys it so much."

"We should open the window," said Tony. "Maybe a nightingale will fly in, or a canary. I read somewhere that they're drawn to beautiful singing."

"Beautiful singink," Mr. Brisch repeated, plainly

flattered. Tony had meant beautiful singing in general, of course, but Mr. Brisch took it to be about him. To be praised for his violin playing, or winning a new convert to communism, had never made him that happy. But for Tony to compliment him on the way he sang "Broken-Down Oven" put him in a state of near rapture.

"You like animals fery much, don't you, Tony?" he said. "I haf seen you vatchink zose flies. You also treat ze fleas fery gently, I see. Are you a member of ze society for ze prevention of cruelty to animals?"

"No," said Tony. "I didn't know there was such a thing."

"They have them in nearly every capital of Europe," Professor Steinbach said.

"Huh," said Tony, pondering the idea. If they had them in every capital of Europe, why not here? The ghetto wasn't a capital, but it certainly was international. As Mr. Glaser and Sons liked to say, all the dregs of Europe were represented in Terezín. Albie Feld even claimed there was an Englishman in the camp.

"Every Englishman cares first about his dog and only then about his butler," said Tony, thinking out loud. "Even if he doesn't have a dog here in the ghetto—or a butler, for that matter—I'm sure he would join the society. Of course, first someone would have to found one."

"Vell, go on zen, Tony," said Mr. Brisch. "Vhy don't you do it yourself?"

"And whom would he protect?" Mr. Abeles said. "As far as I know, there are no animals in the ghetto. Only Jews."

"The Hannover Barracks used to have a horse," said Mr. Glaser and Sons. "But it died of dysentery. I remember, because that was when I stopped eating rotten potatoes."

"That's right, you always have to take the opposite side, don't you?" said Mr. Abeles. Putting on an insulted air, he stormed off to the toilet.

"In the ghetto," said Professor Steinbach after Abeles had left, "horses' work is done by men. They even hitch them to the wagons."

"No one gets too worn out, though," said Mr. Löwy. "I've done it. Usually the wagon is empty and half the men just hold on while they walk alongside."

"Would you mind telling me how the wagon moves, then?" said Mr. Glaser and Sons.

"Usually it's going downhill," said Mr. Löwy.

Tony laughed, imagining the men chasing after the wagon as it sped away from them. Then he realized there were no steep hills in the ghetto. Maybe they pulled the wagon up onto the ramparts. But why would they bother dragging an empty wagon up there? he wondered. Why not? he answered himself. It didn't make any sense to drag it all over the ghetto either.

"What's so funny?" said Mr. Glaser and Sons. "Pulling a wagon is humiliating work."

"You don't pull anysink," said Mr. Brisch. "Mr. Löwy pulls and he is not humiliatink. Your aversion to manual labor demonstrates how you are trapped by your class perspective."

"Oh, please," said Mr. Glaser and Sons. "Everyone here is equal. We all have TB."

"Zere is an enormous difference in classes, efen betveen people viss tuberculosis," said Mr. Brisch. "Betveen you and me, for example. I get it as a proletarian musician in ze Weimark Republic. And you get it as a Jew under Hitler. Because you are carryink sacks and sveatink and sveatink, because you are a spoiled capitalist. But Tony, zis society, ziss is a good idea. Ve have to activate ze Jews. Vhat is wrong, Nurse Anna?" he asked the nurse as she entered the room with a man at her side. She looked upset.

"Where is Mr. Abeles?" she asked.

"He isn't here," said Mr. Brisch.

"I've got him down on my list," said the man with Nurse Anna, glancing at his notepad. "Arnold Abeles, transport number Ba 741, building L 315, room 26. That's here, isn't it?"

"Mr. Abeles left," said Mr. Löwy.

"I had a feeling something would be wrong," said Nurse Anna. "Things always go wrong on my shift. Everything's fine when Nurse Lili or Nurse Maria Louisa are on. But whenever I'm here, there's trouble."

There was some truth to what she said. The last time Nurse Anna had been on duty, Professor Steinbach knocked a syringe to the floor. The time before that, Mr. Brisch was sick to his stomach.

"What do you want him for, anyway?" Mr. Löwy asked. "Can we give him a message?"

"No," said the man. "I need his signature on the transport summons."

"You're kidding," said Mr. Brisch.

"That can't be," said Mr. Löwy.

The men were surprised. Not that they weren't aware there was a transport leaving. They knew that, of course. And it wasn't as if they didn't think it could happen to them. But they had assumed that anyone with tuberculosis would be passed over. Jaundice or cancer didn't offer any protection, but tuberculosis, diphtheria, and scarlet fever had all worked up until now.

"Are you sure there's no mistake?" said Mr. Glaser and Sons. "Mr. Abeles has TB. He's on the Schutzliste."[2]

2) The Schutzlisten ("protection lists") contained the names of

23

"Yes, I know," said the man. "All I have here is 'Mr. Abeles from Kolín, transport number Ba 741, L 315, room 26, is to report,' et cetera, et cetera."

You could tell by looking at him that was really all he knew. No one had told the man a thing, and insofar as a shammes from the Ältestenrat[3] could afford to, he felt sorry for Mr. Abeles.

"I wonder if I have the right man? I'd better double-check," he said. "It would be a shame for someone else to have to go through all that, only to find out in the end they weren't going anywhere."

Things like that happened all the time, and not only when it came to transports. Mr. Löwy, for instance, knew a Mr. Fischmann from České Budějovice who, on March 16, 1939, had received a visit from a man with orders to confiscate his liqueur factory. Along with the keys to his office, the man had carted off three hundred bottles of liqueur and two casks of spirits. Later it came to light that the man had been an impostor

people who were supposedly protected from the transports. But since nobody knew who put together the transport lists, of course nobody knew who put together the protection lists either. It was also entirely possible that there were no protection lists at all.
3) The Ältestenrat (Jewish Council of Elders) pretended to run the ghetto, even though it didn't. Depending on the situation, it also sometimes pretended that it didn't run it when it did.

and the whole thing was a hoax. Of course, eventually Mr. Fischmann lost his factory anyway, but no one could take away his joy on learning that the man was a fraud.

Or take Mr. Glaser and Sons. He knew a Mrs. Friedlender from Prague whose husband had been taken away by the Gestapo. About a week later, she received an urn. She wept over her husband, clothed herself in black, and then suddenly one day Mr. Friedlender turned up at home, alive and well. Together they went to Chotek Gardens and dumped out the urn. Eventually they ended up on a transport to Lodz, but that's another story.

The men in L 315 knew plenty of stories like this, and all their talk was making Nurse Anna nervous.

"That's all well and good," she said, "but where is Mr. Abeles?"

"He went to the toilet," said Mr. Brisch.

Nurse Anna breathed a sigh of relief. "I'm glad to hear," she said. "I was starting to think he really had left. The head nurse would have been furious."

"No," said Professor Steinbach, "he really did go to the toilet."

"I hope he won't be too long," said the man. "I have a few more summonses to take care of still."

He doesn't know Mr. Abeles very well, Tony thought.

Sometimes he takes an hour. Especially if he's consti-pated. Tony turned his thoughts to Ernie, who was going to visit first thing tomorrow. He knew his friend would love the idea of starting an SPCA.

Ernie Jelínek lived in a garret over the Engineers' Barracks. To build a place like that in the ghetto was a luxury. It took a lot of wood and a lot of chutzpah.

But it was an especially elegant brand of chutzpah, unique in the ghetto to cooks, butchers, bakers, and the boys from the Kleiderkammer;[4] a chutzpah founded in the awareness that any one of them was capable, at any time, of offering any member of the Ältestenrat in Magdeburg Barracks a pot of soup or a dumpling.

Ernie was a cook and a close friend of Tony's. The two of them had known each other since Tony was a little boy. When they first came to the ghetto, they had lived together in the hallway of the Sudeten Barracks, camped out on a straw mattress, on the floor. The old men complained that there was a draft, but the boys weren't bothered. They thought it was funny that everyone else had to step over them. Sometimes they even stretched out their legs on purpose, so people would trip over them, and bet on who would trip the most times. But then they moved in with the old men in

4) Clothing Depot, the place for sorting clothes confiscated from new arrivals to the ghetto and collected from inmates who left on the transports.

Hannover Barracks, and that was no fun at all. The old men hacked and wheezed, and the only distraction the two of them had was slipping somebody's hairbrush or shoes under their sheets every once in a while. Usually, though, the old men just found them right away, and didn't even make a fuss. Ernie said it was because they used up all their energy arguing among themselves. He was probably right.

Then Tony got sick and was transferred to L 315, and Ernie moved up in the world, setting up shop in the garret, together with Ledecký.

Of course, depending on how you looked at it, Tony had also moved up in the world. The room he shared with the five old men was just as comfortable as Ernie's place. Only no one else would admit it. In fact, everyone felt sorry for Tony because he had to live in the hospital. People are strange when it comes to some things.

To get to Ernie's garret, you had to walk through two large halls full of old men. In the first, Tony had a friend, Mr. Kohn, who used to occupy the bed where Mr. Glaser and Sons now lay. He had been released from L 315 when his tuberculosis, as Nurse Anna put it, "settled down."

Tony used to bring him books from the men in room 26. Usually, Mr. Kohn didn't bother to read them, but he always had plenty to say about them. Mr. Kohn liked to criticize.

"So, boy, are you bringing me another book from Mr. Löwy?" he said as Tony passed through on his way to Ernie's place.

"No," said Tony. "I'm going to see Ernie. You wouldn't happen to know if he's home, would you?"

"How should I know?" said Mr. Kohn. "It's no concern of mine. If you want my opinion, though, if he isn't in the kitchen, he's probably in the attic. Then again, he might be somewhere else."

Then Mr. Kohn turned to his usual topic of conversation: books.

"Pardon me, son, but could you tell Mr. Löwy not to send me any more books like that last one? Books like that I can do without."

"I'll tell him," said Tony. Normally he would have asked Mr. Kohn why he didn't like it, but today he was in a hurry.

Noticing this, Mr. Kohn launched into his grouch routine. "You think you're smart, don't you?" he said. "All the young people today think they're so smart. Especially young Jews. That's why I don't like them, or old Jews, either. Especially not them! How could Mr. Löwy send me such a book, tell me that!"

"I'm sure he didn't do it on purpose," said Tony. "He must have thought you would like it."

"How could I like *Five Weeks in a Balloon*?" said Mr. Kohn. "The worries some people have."

Tony had enjoyed the book, so he continued to stick up for Mr. Löwy.

"You're Jewish, too, Mr. Kohn," he said.

"And what of it?" said Mr. Kohn. "What is that supposed to mean?"

"Well, if you're a Jew, you can't hate Jews."

Tony, lacking experience, subscribed to the widespread but mistaken belief that Jews couldn't hate other Jews, Czechs other Czechs, Frenchmen other Frenchmen, and so on. But the reality is they can. And often do. Philosophers and other misguided souls offer all sorts of complicated explanations for this phenomenon, most of them based on the idea of self-hatred. Some disciples of Freud interpret it as hatred for one's mother or father, resulting in a complex. In reality, however, the explanation is quite simple: Czechs have more contact with Czechs than anyone else; French with French; and Jews with Jews. Mr. Kohn was far from the only anti-Semite in the ghetto. In fact, one could even say their numbers were growing by the day.

"The Jews," said Mr. Kohn, "aren't even a real nation. No wonder Hitler hates them so much. In fact, I'd be surprised if he left them alone. He'd have to be cracked in the head. Take that book Mr. Löwy sent me. What serious businessman would take five weeks off from work to fly around in some silly balloon?"

"But it isn't only Jews that Hitler doesn't like," Tony said. He had no illusions of changing Mr. Kohn's mind, but he felt he had to say something.

"The reason Hitler doesn't like all those other people," said Mr. Kohn, "is because they're even worse than the Jews."

"So you think the Germans are best?"

"The Germans are the worst of them all," said Mr. Kohn. "Right after the Hungarians. It's Bismarck's fault, and William the II's, plus the fact that they're Lutherans. Lutherans are even worse than Catholics. Although the Catholics are a pretty gamey lot themselves. Orthodox Christians, too. They're all anti-Semites. But Mr. Löwy takes the cake. Can you imagine me being so crude as to send him *Five Weeks in a Balloon*?"

Tony didn't quite understand. But he had the impression Mr. Kohn was voicing feelings rather than thoughts. And his feelings had no logic to them, that much was clear. The question is, Tony thought, is it even possible for feelings to have logic, and if Mr. Kohn's feelings had any logic, would they still be feelings then? So instead he asked again whether Mr. Kohn had seen

Ernie, and if he hadn't, had anyone else gone up to the attic?

Mr. Kohn again replied that he didn't know, Ernie wasn't his problem, but if anyone besides Ernie had gone up there, it must have been some chonte, seeing as no decent girl would go up to the attic with Ernie, and that Ernie was a ganef, seeing as no decent boy would be dragging girls up there, but he didn't know if any girl had gone up there, but if she had, she probably went in the back way, though she might have passed this way too, since it wasn't as if he noticed every single person who happened to wander past, and even if he did, he certainly wouldn't have noticed any ganef or chonte.

Tony—who knew ganef meant something like "scoundrel" in Jewish, but didn't know what a chonte was and was too embarrassed to ask—thanked Mr. Kohn for the information and made his way out through the bunks and into the other room. He then walked through a series of corridors, up a flight of stairs, and climbed the ladder to the attic to see if Ernie was home.

The door was locked.

Tony knocked gently.

"Who is it?" said a female voice.

"It's me," said Tony. He wasn't surprised Ernie had a girl in there. In fact, he would have been surprised if he didn't. But in that respect, Ernie rarely surprised him.

Tony heard Ernie say, "It's my buddy, he's a great kid."

That made Tony happy. See how nice Ernie talks about me when I'm not around, he thought.

He heard Ernie and the girl exchange a few quiet words, then Ernie asked what he wanted. Tony, speaking through the door, told his friend he had an idea but couldn't say what it was. He didn't want to just burst right out with the idea of an SPCA in front of the girl. Who knew what she might think? What if she didn't like animals?

Then he heard Ernie say, "He's just a little kid, but he comes up with some really terrific ideas sometimes. Go let him in."

I guess he remembers how last summer I suggested having races rolling down the roof of the Magdeburg Barracks, Tony thought. In the end, it didn't happen, after Ledecký said someone might roll off into the gutter, but it couldn't have been such a bad idea if Ernie still remembered it.

Or maybe he was thinking of last New Year's, when I came up with all those funny names for the guys. Tony had translated Albie's last name into Czech, for instance, making him Albie Pole. (That was Tony's personal favorite.)

But the girl didn't seem interested in Tony's ideas.

She didn't want to open the door, and Ernie was probably on the top bunk and didn't feel like climbing down.

Tony sympathized. It was no mean feat climbing down from the top bunk. That was the one drawback. The great thing was, you could throw stuff down at the person underneath you. But getting up in the morning was tough. It was never fun getting up in the morning, but doing it from the top bunk was especially unpleasant.

Again he heard Ernie sweet-talking the girl: "Go open the door and I'll make us some coffee," he said.[5]

She announced that she didn't want any coffee and she wasn't about to climb down on account of some harebrained idea.

"It isn't harebrained," Tony said, still speaking through the door. "We want to found a society for the prevention of cruelty to animals."

He hadn't wanted to give it away, but he felt he had no choice. Otherwise the girl might have sat there an hour.

Just as he expected, though, her reaction to his explanation was less than positive. Maybe she really didn't like animals.

5) "Coffee" in the ghetto meant a cup of hot water colored with chicory. But sometimes even that was enough to give you a boost.

"Pardon me, but who do you plan to protect?" she said. "There are no animals here."

"At first, we were thinking the horse," said Tony, "but turns out it died of dysentery."

Ernie was touched. "There, you see?" he said to the girl. "That poor horse died of dysentery, and here you are, lazing around. Go let him in."

But she wouldn't budge.

"I don't intend to parade around naked in front of some boy," she said.

"OK, I guess you're right," said Ernie. "Tony, why don't you come back some other time. Like maybe tomorrow."

"I don't mind waiting," said Tony. "My mom walks around in front of me without clothes all the time. Tell her to put her clothes on, if she wants. I can wait."

"Hey," Ernie said, "did you ever think about mice? There's tons of them here. Rats, too."

"Yeah, I thought of that," said Tony. "But I didn't want to decide without you."

"Just tell her to get dressed," Tony repeated, now almost begging. It didn't seem right to talk about it through the door, and besides, he was getting cold.

"I'm not going to put anything on," said the girl. "It's too hot."

"That's true," said Ernie. "We've got it nice and toasty in here."

"I don't care if she doesn't get dressed," said Tony. "Just as long as she opens the door."

The two on the other side of the door had another exchange of words.

"The air in here's getting pretty bad, anyway," said Ernie. "At least he could open the window."

But the girl remained skeptical. "Oh, come on, he can't even reach that high."

"Sure, I can," said Tony. "I'm five foot five. Plus I can stand on the stool. But first you've got to let me in."

"That's true," said Ernie. "He always opens the window for us. Go let him in. Really, he's a great kid."

"All right, if it means that much to you," said the girl.

Tony heard her climb out of the bunk, hop down, and pad across the floor in her bare feet. But he was taken aback when the door opened and he found himself staring at Nurse Lili from L 315.

Apart from that, she looked exactly the same as any other naked woman. And she wasn't a bit embarrassed.

"Hi," was all she said.

"Hi," said Tony.

"Howdy do," said Ernie.

"I guess I'll come back some other time," said Tony

once they had dispensed with their greetings. "I didn't mean to interrupt."

He was being honest. Before he found out that it was Nurse Lili, he'd been happy to interrupt them. But now that he knew, he felt bad. He knew how little time Nurse Lili had to herself.

Ernie didn't seem to mind at all, though. "You're not interrupting," he said. "We were already done, weren't we, Lil?"

"If you say so," said Nurse Lili. She climbed back up into the bunk.

Tony noticed how agile she was. As if she climbed in and out of the bunk every day. And yet in L 315 she had an ordinary bed. Ernie had a bunk bed because he shared the room with Ledecký, who wasn't there at the moment.

Otherwise, the place was furnished like any other attic. Apart from the bunks, there was a stove and a sink. Next to the bunks, Ernie had hung a reproduction of a painting of Van Gogh.

Tony liked the picture of the blue man with the yellow hair. He looked kind of like Ernie. Whenever Tony came to the attic and looked at the picture, he had a feeling that the man in it was looking back at him. But it was probably just an illusion. After all, it was only a picture.

It was funny to see Nurse Lili sitting on Ernie's bunk. The next time she gives me a calcium shot, Tony thought, I'll remember this. Maybe then it won't be so bad. Then again, calcium's always bad—the way the heat slowly rises from your feet to your head. Some people claimed it was the other way around, and it sank from your head to your feet. But they were wrong. Some people don't know what they're talking about.

"So what's the deal with the animals?" Ernie said, sitting up.

He sat on the edge of the bunk, legs hanging down, so Tony could see he was wearing blue undershorts. That was a relief. It would have been disturbing to see Ernie with nothing on in front of Nurse Lili, even if she was a nurse. With her it was different; she was a woman. But to see Ernie naked would have taken him down a notch in Tony's eyes.

"Every city in Europe has an SPCA," said Tony. "That's what Professor Steinbach said."

"He's got a point," said Ernie. "Though it's not as if we've got a lot of animals around here. Lil's right about that. There aren't even any dogs."

"And we use men instead of horses," said Tony. "Mr. Löwy said that." Tony was very careful not to present others' thoughts as his own. He always cited the author.

"Right," said Ernie, even though he wasn't sure what Tony was talking about. He only knew Mr. Löwy by sight. "Anyway, there's lots of animals here that no one takes care of. Like all those mice, for instance."

"Nobody ever takes care of them," said Nurse Lili.

"How would you know?" said Ernie. "I think people take care of them everywhere. Except here, that is. The only thing we take care of here is orphans, retards, and old fogies. But we don't pay any attention to mice."

"Old people need someone to take care of them, or else they'd kick the bucket."

Nurse Lili was speaking as a professional.

But Ernie wouldn't give up. Apparently, he viewed her more as a woman than as a nurse. "If only," he said. "The way those old goats in the Altersheim[6] scream and shout all the time, they seem pretty lively to me."

"They are," said Nurse Lili. "And so are the ones in L 315. Mr. Adamson, for instance. And he's religious, too."

"How do you know?" said Ernie. "You can't tell just by looking at someone."

6) The Altersheim (Old Age Home) housed the old folks in the ghetto. Unlike the Jugendheim (Youth Home), they didn't receive extra rations. The Germans said old-timers didn't need it, since they weren't growing anymore.

"I can," said Nurse Lili brightly. "Number one, he's always praying. Number two, he always trades me his ground meat for my potatoes. He says he's afraid there might be pork in it."

"You little vixen," Ernie said. "Come here and let me give you a spanking." She tried to fend him off, but in vain.

Tony giggled when he saw Lili's rear end, picturing himself giving her a shot. Though he wasn't exactly sure how. He just knew there were three types: epidermal, intravenous, and intramuscular. Epidermals were no big deal. Anyone could learn how to give them. But an intravenous shot, into the vein, that was no joke. Especially if the person had a bad vein. The hardest one of all, though, was the intramuscular, into the rear end. You had to be careful not to hit a nerve. But all the nurses seemed to enjoy giving them. Even Nurse Maria Louisa, the ex-nun, whose morals were beyond reproach. Tony began to understand the attraction. Maybe he would enjoy it, too.

"What are you laughing at?" said Nurse Lili. Apparently, she took her rear end seriously.

Ernie stuck up for Tony. "Sometimes life is beautiful," he said. "Why shouldn't he laugh?"

"It doesn't look that beautiful to me," said Nurse Lili.

"Maybe that's because it's so dark in here," said Ernie. "Tony, go pull down the blackout shade and turn on the light."

"But I'm not dressed yet," said Nurse Lili.

"I think he's already seen you," said Ernie.

"All right, if you say so," said Nurse Lili.

Clambering up on the stool, Tony pulled down the shade and switched on the light, while Nurse Lili hopped down from the bunk and began to get dressed. Now, in the light, Tony noticed that her figure was almost exactly the same as his mother's. Only her breasts were a little bigger.

"Nice, huh?" said Ernie.

"I wouldn't know," said Tony. "I don't have any experience."

"Aw, go on," said Ernie. "You're supposed to say you've had your way with Marlene Dietrich and Greta Garbo, at least."

"But I haven't," said Tony. "I don't even know them, so why would I say that? I don't like it when people lie."

"It's not a lie," said Ernie. "It's a biological need to exaggerate."

"I guess I just don't have it," said Tony, getting a little angry. He thought highly of Ernie, but not when he said stupid stuff like that.

"Don't worry," said Nurse Lili. "Ernie has a biological need to shoot off his mouth today."

"And so what if I do?" said Ernie. "What if I'm fed up with all this? What if I need to get it off my chest?"

"Trouble in the kitchen again?" Tony asked.

"Nope. Everything under control in Q 206," said Ernie. "There's trouble there all the time. You get used to it. It's just that the world is starting to get on my nerves. Know what I mean? I can't complain. I've got everything I can think of. Grub, girls, this attic. People respect me for being a cook. I even get to take time off every once in a while. But it's just no fun anymore. What does it all mean? *That* is the question."

Some people might have been surprised to hear *Hamlet* quoted from the mouth of a cook. In the ghetto, though, it was normal. All the cooks had at least a high school education. They wouldn't have put up with anyone who was uneducated. Then again, they wouldn't put up with anyone who was *too* educated, either. Lawyers, doctors, philosophers—none of them stood a chance of getting a job in the kitchen.

"Maybe it would be better if we had an SPCA," said Tony. "At least then there'd be something happening."

"That's true," said Ernie. "Was it your idea?"

"Yeah. Actually, no," said Tony. "I was inspired by Mr. Abeles. You know how mad he gets when Mr. Brisch and I sing."

"Oh, I know," said Ernie. "It isn't nice to tease old men. They can't defend themselves. They're like animals that way."

"No, but I stopped," said Tony. "Because right after that, he got a summons for the transport. But when he asked me to sing 'Little White Dove,' it made me think. I tried to imagine what would happen if a pigeon flew in our window. Or if I brought a chicken into our room. Know what I mean? I wouldn't even mind if it made its nest next to my bed. I'm hardly ever there. I spend all day roaming around the building."

"They say chickens are filthy," said Ernie.

"Mine would be clean," said Tony. "I'd raise it to be that way. I'm serious. It's all a question of upbringing, trust me. Ever since I was little, I've had to wash my hands before meals. And now, if I don't wash them, I can hardly stand to eat."

"Just as long as it doesn't cackle too much," Ernie said. "Chickens do that, you know? These days even chickens are nervous. Besides, how are we going to find a rooster here in the ghetto?"

"We might be able to scare one up," said Tony.

"Have you lost your minds?" said Nurse Lili. Meanwhile she had gotten dressed. "You aren't allowed to raise poultry in the ghetto."

"So what?" said Ernie. "We do a lot of things that aren't allowed."

"Yeah, right," said Nurse Lili, slapping his hand away. "But Jews weren't allowed to raise poultry even before. Not even when they had meat rations. The last time I saw a goose was 1938."

"Well, you may be seeing one again soon," said Ernie. "If we form our society. You know what?" he said, turning to Tony, "let's call the boys over and see what they think."

"Fantastic," said Tony. And he did a somersault for joy. It wasn't a very good one, though. There wasn't enough room in the attic to do a good one.

Three days later, they gathered at the coffeehouse. Albie Feld, the Kleiderkammer goalkeeper; Ledecký the cook, Ernie's roommate from Q 206; Jenda Schleim, the butcher and actor; Tony's mother, Liza; Ernie; Nurse Lili; and Tony. Nurse Lili was meeting everyone for the first time.

Ernie didn't bother to introduce her.

He had announced in advance she would come.

Their little expedition was preceded by a meeting during which Tony introduced his proposal to establish a society for the prevention of cruelty to animals. They weren't too thrilled. Albie Feld didn't feel it was dignified for him, the ghetto's top goalkeeper, who had contact on a daily basis with the leaders of the Ältestenrat, to be concerned with animals. Jenda Schleim also didn't much like it at first. It wasn't until Ledecký expressed doubts that Jenda took an interest. That of course set Ledecký against it, though he restrained himself for Tony's sake, and given that Liza, being Tony's mother, was in favor, Albie Feld also felt obliged not to oppose it. In the end, they all agreed it might actually be fun, and Ledecký said there were pigeons nesting in the church on the town square and suggested they go have a look at them.

Everyone agreed to put him in charge, but seeing that it was already late and the pigeons would probably be asleep, they decided to postpone their trip until the next day.

Tony was so excited he jumped up and down, waving his arms around and grinning at his mother.

She worked as an inspector at the kitchen in Q 206. It wasn't quite as lucrative as cooking. In the ghetto there was an unwritten law that cooks, bakers, and butchers were allowed to steal more than anyone else. Inspectors could steal, but not as much.

What really made Tony proud of her, though, was she went around with the boys.

Most of them were ten or twelve years younger than she was. But you wouldn't have known it to look at her. Especially when she wore pants.

At the moment, she had on a skirt. Albie Feld had his arm around her waist. Tony didn't mind. He liked Albie. Some people accused him of being a ladies' man, but nobody could deny he was the best goalie in the ghetto. Definitely a class up from Mahrer, who played for the Bakers. But apparently Tony's mother didn't find it appropriate. "If you don't mind," she said, "could you kindly put your paws elsewhere?"

"Where would you like me to put them?" said Albie. "If you could kindly be specific."

"Wherever you want, so long as they're off of me. You've got hands like a gorilla."

He sure does, Tony thought with admiration. Nobody else in the ghetto could make a diving save like Albie.

Meanwhile the group had made their way across the town square and now stood before the church.

It was the only uninhabited building in the ghetto. The gate and windows were boarded shut, but there were two small windows open in the bell tower. That was how the pigeons had gotten in.

Instead of entering the church directly, Ledecký led them into the small chapel attached to it. The area around the chapel was one of the few spots in the ghetto where grass grew in the summer. Now, of course, it was just mud. Like everywhere else.

"Yuck," said Jenda Schleim. "My boots are going to get totally soaked. And tomorrow I'm playing Macduff."

He never missed a chance to stress the fact that he was not only a butcher, but also an actor.

Jenda came from a normal family. His father was a physician, or something like that. Jenda had gone to a good high school, but flunked Latin, so he transferred to a business academy, which he was then forced to leave because of his Jewish origin. After that, he had trained to be a locksmith. It was only here in the ghetto that he became a butcher and an actor. He harbored a high opinion of his acting skills, but most everyone else still saw him as just a plain old butcher.

"It's dry inside," said Ledecký. He pried loose a few boards and stepped aside. "Ladies first."

"I can't," said Tony's mother. "Not in a skirt."

"I can't either," said Nurse Lili, even though she was wearing pants. She must have had other reasons.

"Pity," said Albie Feld. "I was looking forward to the view. But if the ladies won't go first, I will. The dark doesn't scare me."

He stepped through the gap and the others followed behind him.

Ledecký led them down a long corridor. It was pitch black and they walked pressed closely together. Still, even Albie didn't take any liberties. Maybe, what with the dark, he was afraid he might accidentally grope one of the boys instead.

Once they got inside, Ledecký handed out candles. There weren't enough, so Tony and Nurse Lili didn't get one. "Damn it," said Ledecký. "I could have sworn I had twice as many."

But none of the others gave it a second thought, and Tony and Lili didn't mind. Everybody ran around, casting huge shadows against the walls, in fascinating patterns.

Tony was captivated.

The inside of the church was much bigger and taller than the Schleusse, the room in the Reitschule where the Germans confiscated the belongings of the people who arrived in the ghetto on the transports. And that room held three hundred.

The biggest room Tony had ever seen in his life was the concourse at the Woodrow Wilson Train Station, in Prague. But that was a long time ago, and they didn't have any paintings on the walls there. Besides, the train station was noisy, and here it was unbelievably quiet.

Jenda and Ledecký started to argue about something, but soon fell silent again. Even Tony's mother was quiet.

Tony walked around the church, looking at the paintings.

He actually couldn't see them that well, but with Ledecký and Jenda using the candles to try and find the pigeons, which were probably nesting up near the ceiling, he managed to catch a glimpse or two.

Then Albie pulled out his flashlight, and that was even better.

Most of the paintings were scenes of animals. Only a few of them showed people.

But they all looked sort of freckled. Almost like Ernie.

"Who's that pale man on the cross?" Tony asked.

"That's Jesus of Nazareth," his mother said. "Jesus Christ."

"Why does everyone around him look so upset?" Tony asked.

"You think they should be glad to see him crucified?" said Albie. "You think it's nice, hanging up there on a cross like that? His muscles must have hurt like crazy. If you've ever tried any gymnastics, like the rings, you know what I mean."

Tony didn't find that explanation too helpful, so he turned to his mother.

"Who is that lady next to him?" he asked.

"That's Jesus' mother. The Virgin Mary."

"Huh," said Tony. "So why did they crucify him, anyway?"

"Well, he was sort of a Jewish gadfly," said Albie. "He kept saying things people didn't like."

"He decided he'd rather be crucified than take back what he said," said Ernie.

"Like what?" said Tony.

"His beliefs," said Ernie.

"Oh, I get it," said Tony. "So he was kind of like Masaryk."

"No, not at all," said Albie. "Jesus was just an ordinary stubborn-headed Jew."

"But he did convince all those other people," Ernie said.

"Only because he got crucified, though," Ledecký chimed in.

"Huh," Tony said. The whole thing was still pretty fuzzy to him. But whatever the case, he sensed that the pale man deserved his respect. Tony always deferred to Ernie when it came to matters like this.

Everyone in the group stopped and thought about it a minute. Whatever class they came from, whatever their family status: Albie, son of a lawyer; Jenda, son of a doctor; Nurse Lili, daughter of a shop owner; and Ledecký, child of aristocrats—all of them, daughters and sons of the modern age. The idea that people used to be crucified over religious differences struck them as bizarre.

Finally, Jenda Schleim broke the silence.

"So where are the pigeons?" he said. "I don't see any."

"There, over the fresco of the Virgin Mary, there's a nest. And there, over St. Joseph, there's another," Ledecký said.

But he didn't sound too sure of himself.

Everyone found it strange that there weren't any birds flying around or cooing, after hearing Ledecký talk about them so enthusiastically.

"I wonder if they're sick," Nurse Lili said with a note of concern.

They looked around the two spots with the flashlight, but couldn't find a single trace. Not even a nest.

They had a hard time imagining the birds had left so suddenly. Even assuming their instinct had warned them and they had gone away (although what kind of instinct would that be, to warn them from a society for the prevention of cruelty to animals), it didn't seem likely that they would have taken their nests with them. Pigeons didn't do that, or any other birds.

"I don't see a single pigeon," said Jenda Schleim again. "I wonder if someone's trying to play a joke on us." And in case there was any doubt as to who he considered responsible, he took a step toward Ledecký. "I wonder," he said, "if that someone isn't just using the pigeons as an excuse to drag us into a Catholic church. So he can convert us to the true faith."

He was referring not only to Ledecký's comment about Jesus, but also to the fact that Ledecký came from an old Catholic family of aristocrats. One of his great-grandfathers had married a Jewish woman and converted to Judaism. Even though Ledecký's grandfather had returned to the Catholic faith, under the Nuremberg Laws Ledecký was still considered a Jew.

"Oh, please," Ledecký said. "This church hasn't even been consecrated."

"That doesn't prove a thing," Jenda said. Ledecký got on his nerves. Whenever he played an aristocrat, he acted like Cyrano de Bergerac. Ledecký was a living reminder that not every nobleman looked like an actor from the National Theater. And that disturbed his fragile self-image.

"Looks like somebody made a mess," said Ledecký. "Look at that." He shone his flashlight on some piles of pigeon feces. It was splattered all over the place. Even the painting of the Virgin Mary had been defiled. That was what made everything look freckled.

"I'll second that," said Ernie. "Somebody made a mess all right."

"There used to be a nest right over the Madonna," said Ledecký. They poked around for the pigeons a little while longer until finally Ledecký announced it was time to give up. "Listen," he said, "I think I know what happened. The last time, as I was leaving, that bratty Tausik kid saw me. I'd bet anything he told his brother, and his parents came in here and chased the pigeons away."

"I propose we send a delegation to go give them a piece of our minds," said Albie Feld.

"I'll second that," said Ernie. "But there's twice as

59

many of them as there are of us, and they're all strong as oxes."

"Fine, suit yourself," said Albie. "Just don't shit your pants."

Tony was starting to get mad at him.

Albie spoke that way often. Usually Tony didn't care, but here, in the church, with his voice resounding the way it did, it struck him as inappropriate.

He had a hunch Ernie felt the same way.

"No one's afraid of the Tausiks," said Ernie. "But no one wants to fight if they don't have to, either. Besides, the pigeons are probably all dead by now."

"I agree," Tony said quietly. "They would have been hard to protect anyway."

"I'm curious to see just who you all plan to protect then," said Albie Feld.

He sounded angry. But Tony knew him. He would get over it in a minute.

"We'll find someone," said Jenda, using a gesture everyone recognized from his performance in *The Robbers*. He had played the idealist Franz Moor. Sometimes he not only gestured like him, but even tried to act like him. "It isn't easy," Jenda said. "Franz Moor was dealing with robbers, but I'm surrounded by scoundrels."

This was both true and untrue. As Mr. Löwy used to say, who could you call a scoundrel in the ghetto?

Who was more of one and less of one? Was Pašeles from L 262 more of one, for promising Mr. Löwy he would steal three potatoes for him, then bringing him two and claiming that he had lost one, even though Mr. Löwy knew full well that scoundrel Pašeles had traded one of his potatoes to that scoundrel Lederer from Q 28 for two puffs of his cigarette? Or was that scoundrel Lederer more of a scoundrel, for eating the potato that scoundrel Pašeles had traded him, even though he knew full well it had been stolen and that that scoundrel Pašeles was supposed to give it to Mr. Löwy? Hard to say. Only one thing was certain: There weren't many scoundrels in the ghetto who were truly decent people.

On the other hand, lots of people in the ghetto had a good heart.

Take, for instance, Jenda Schleim.

Or Ledecký.

Or even Albie Feld.

If they hadn't had a good heart, they would have given up after failing to find any pigeons in the church. But instead they came up with a new plan, right there on the spot.

"Maybe we could take care of lions and elephants?" said Albie, shining his flashlight on Noah's Ark.

"It should probably be some small animal," said Ernie.

"Lice," said Albie. "We could set up preserves for them. Every woman's got one. Hey, Liza. Show me your preserve." He lifted up the hem of Liza's skirt.

"You're terrible," said Liza, pushing him away.

He may be an excellent keeper, thought Tony. Especially when it comes to diving saves, he's the best in the ghetto, hands down. But he's got zero tact.

"It should probably be some domestic animal," said Ernie.

"How about fleas?" said Tony. "They're a lot more likeable than lice. And they're domestic, right?"

"Definitely," said Ledecký. "There's just one problem: How are you going to breed them?"

"I've got a big jar in L 315," said Tony. "So far, we've just been using it to drown them." He realized it sounded barbaric. But if they poured out the water, they could easily raise them in there. There was probably room for twenty fleas, he reckoned.

"And what would you feed them?" Nurse Lili asked.

Tony wasn't put off. He had the whole thing figured out.

"I'd give them a little blood after the sedimentation tests."

Some of you may be shocked by the casualness with which Tony discussed the liquid known as human blood. But consider the fact that it was Jewish blood.

Not to mention, how was he supposed to respect Mr. Löwy's blood when every time he had it drawn he would grumble, "Um Gottes willen, Nurse, did you have to use the dull needle again? You know I have a bad vein. With a needle that dull you couldn't even get into Mr. Brisch, and his veins are excellent. How do you expect to get into mine, when you know how bad they are? For crying out loud!" How was Tony supposed to respect the blood of Mr. Glaser and Sons, when every time he was scheduled for a sedimentation test, he hid in the toilet, claiming he had diarrhea, even when everyone knew he'd been constipated the past two days? Now, the blood of Professor Steinbach or Mr. Brisch, that Tony respected. But they didn't take their blood that often.

"Actually," said Ernie, "when I said 'domestic animals,' I had something else in mind. More like cats and dogs, or geese."

"I don't like geese," said Nurse Lili. "They honk and bite."

"I don't like geese either," said Albie. When he said "geese," he clearly had a certain type of woman in mind.

Albie's way of expressing himself was getting less and less appealing to Tony every day. There was no need for a goalie of his caliber to talk like that. He should have left the double entendres to Max Schumacher,

from the Vienna team, who let in every second shot. Albie Feld was the best keeper in the ghetto. By way of explanation, we note here that besides teams based on profession—Butchers, Bakers, Cooks, Kleiderkammer—the ghetto league also had city and national sides: Germany, Vienna, Holland, Denmark, Pilsen, and so on. But those teams tended not to be as good.

Ledecký chimed in: "You know that little ratter the SS-Sturmbannführer has? He might be worth a try."

"But first we'd have to ghettoize him," Ernie said. By that he meant they'd have to keep the dog out of the Sturmbannführer's sight, since no matter how well they took care of him, the SS man wasn't likely to look very kindly on it. If he spotted them with his dog, he might even shoot. Of course in such a way so as not to wound the dog.

"That can be arranged," said Ledecký. "No pigeons, so we go with the ratter."

Everyone went along with it. After all, he may have blown it with the pigeons, but he hadn't blown it so badly that they didn't think the plan with the ratter would work. They all knew how the Tausiks were, the way they snooped around everywhere. Besides, even if Ledecký was a cook and a former aristocrat, he couldn't have eyes everywhere. There was no way he could've known that those stinkers would report it, though obviously if he'd been a bit more careful, he might have suspected something. Still, as Ernie said, the fact that he blamed himself for it, even just a little, gave them some assurance, even if not a one hundred percent guarantee, that he would be careful when it came to the ratter and do his level best.

Meanwhile they agreed that as long as they were in the church, they might as well have some fun. Given all the open space, Nurse Lili suggested they dance. But they didn't have any music. There was no organ, and even if there had been, it was doubtful whether Albie, though he played a bit of accordion (he had taken piano lessons as a boy), would have known how to play it. He claimed he did, but there was no way to prove it, since there was no organ, and even if it had been true, it was of no use to them. So Ledecký suggested they put on a play.

Jenda Schleim was fiercely opposed. He said it would be a desecration of the art of theater for him to act with people who had never put on a play in their lives, not to mention in a church, of all places.

Ledecký countered that people had put on plays in churches in the Middle Ages and it didn't bother anyone then.

To which Jenda Schleim replied that fortunately they were no longer in the Middle Ages, and as a counterproposal he suggested they perform a little Christian service instead, with Ledecký as the priest. He was of course trying to get Ledecký's goat, but Ledecký didn't fall for it. "I could," he said. "I served many times as an acolyte, so I know all the moves. I don't have a cassock, though."

"Plus we don't have hats," said Tony.

"That's all right," his mother said. "Hats are for synagogue. You don't need them in church."

"Oh," said Tony. "Can women go to church too?"

"Sure," said Liza. "It's just synagogues they can't go to. Or they can, but they have to stand in the balcony. Which isn't to say that Christians treat women any better than Jews."

"I heard that too," said Nurse Lili. "I also heard that Muslims allow polygamy."

"So, don't we?" said Albie Feld. That gave him an idea. "You know what? Let's make Ledecký the priest and he can marry us all. Looks to me like we've got a new addition," he said, tipping his head toward Lili.

Most of the others seemed to agree. But Ernie wasn't convinced.

"What do you mean? You all know Lili."

"But we want to know her more," said Albie, pulling Lili down onto the pew next to him.

"Now hold on," said Liza. "There are children here."

She knew, of course, that Tony was no longer a child. She had always spoken to him like an adult. Sometimes she even treated him like one. But she didn't want him to take part in the festivities. She was afraid he might catch cold.

"We can send the children outside," said Albie.

"Don't you think someone ought to ask me?" said Nurse Lili.

"What is there to ask?" said Albie. "You'll get a pound of potatoes."

"Wait a second," Ernie said. "Lili's not that type of girl. She doesn't want potatoes."

"So we'll give her dumplings then," said Albie. He didn't care either way. As the goalkeeper for the Kleiderkammer, he could afford it.

"I don't give a damn about your dumplings," Lili said.

Liza had reservations too. "I don't know if it's right. Here of all places."

"Why wouldn't it be right?" said Albie. "You know how many people must have been married in here? So what's wrong with a little party?"

"He's got a point," said Ernie.

"If you say so," said Lili.

So Ledecký walked Tony back down the dark hallway, grumbling to himself the whole way. Apparently he wasn't keen on Albie's idea, either. The church was pretty dirty. But Tony's mind was elsewhere. He was in a fantastic mood. This is going to be great, he thought. Our own dog. When we get our rations, I can share my sugar with him. But then he realized the ratter might not eat powdered sugar. Being the SS-Sturmbannführer's dog, he might be spoiled. Maybe he only ate cubes. And there were no cubes in the ghetto. But then he thought about it some more and decided the dog would definitely eat powdered sugar. If he didn't like it, Tony would pour it down his throat. Just like he did himself.

CHAPTER 4

IN WHICH EVERYONE—EVEN TONY—GETS A GOOD SQUARE MEAL

Tony didn't know how the party in the church went after he left. He asked Nurse Lili about it the next day, but she wouldn't say. A few days later, Jenda finally volunteered some information.

"Ledecký served as priest," he said, "and every ten minutes he paired off another two couples. Almost everyone there got a chance to be married to all the girls."

"But a priest can only do weddings, not divorces," Tony said.

Clearly he'd picked up some knowledge from the learned gentlemen in room 26.

"No one really took it that seriously," said Jenda. "Then, at the end, I took over from Ledecký, so he could—"

"So he could what?" Tony asked.

"So he could get married too," Jenda said with some hesitation. Suddenly it dawned on him that Tony was still a boy. "But I wasn't as good at it as him, since I don't really know Latin."

"And Ledecký does?" Tony asked.

"Just a few words," said Jenda, "but he likes to brag. You know how he is. By the way, do you know where Lili is right now?"

Tony told him where he was most likely to find Nurse Lili at that time of day, then asked how the preparations were coming along to kidnap the SS-Sturmbannführer's ratter. But Jenda didn't know. All he cared about was where Nurse Lili was, what was the best way to get there, whether he was allowed to visit right now, did the head doctor usually stop in at this time of day, when did she give shots, when did she hand out pills, etc.

Tony was struck by his sudden interest in the operations of the sick room in L 315.

But once again, Tony simply took note of how variable the boys' interests were. They could be curious about something one day and not care at all the next. He still vividly remembered how his idea for keg-rolling races on the roof of Magdeburg Barracks had ended up, and he was worried it might end up the same with the SS-Sturmbannführer's ratter. This time, however, his concerns turned out to be unfounded.

The next day, after Jenda Schleim came to visit, Tony got a note from Ernie: *Come for ratter this afternoon.* Nurse Maria Louisa was on duty for the afternoon shift, so his bed rest didn't finish a second sooner than it was supposed to.

He walked out at three on the dot.

On the way, he stopped off to see Mr. Kohn. He had a book from Mr. Löwy for him.

"Let's see," said Mr. Kohn. "Hm. *Anna Karenina*. What kind of strange name is that for a firm? *Karenina*. I could see *Karenin Bros.*, or *Karenin and Sons*, or *Karenin and Co*. Any of those would work. But *Anna Karenina*?"

Tony wasn't in the mood for a literary debate, so he made it clear that he had other things on his mind and mentioned the society for the prevention of cruelty to animals. He made sure not to leave out the horse from the Hannover Barracks, who had died of dysentery.

That got Mr. Kohn's attention. "It used to be," he said, "that when a man rode a horse, it gave him dignity. Anyone who didn't have a horse was a nebbish."

"You had a horse, didn't you, Mr. Kohn?"

"Are you kidding? You think a lowly law clerk like me could afford a horse? I never did like people with horses. Or dogs. In my opinion, it was a wise move by the Reichsprotektor to ban people having animals at home. Most Jews spoil their dogs. Not to mention their cats. It's an outrage!"

"Does that mean you would be mad at me if we protect them?" asked Tony. He didn't want to have a falling-out with Mr. Kohn over the SPCA.

"Why should I be mad at you?" said Mr. Kohn. "Someone has to take care of those miserable creatures."

"That's right," said Tony. His thoughts drifted off to what they should name the dog. He liked Buddy, though he also thought Alfred might be good, like Ledecký's Doberman. But then he rejected that too. Too distinguished for a ratter.

He told Mr. Kohn good-bye, left the room, and walked down the hall. As he climbed the ladder to the attic, he perked up his ears for the sound of a bark. But he didn't hear a sound.

All the boys were already there.

Ledecký lay on the top bunk, reigning over the scene. But he didn't look very aristocratic, stuffing his face with food.

The rest of them were sitting around a large aluminum bowl.

"It's about time," said Ernie. "I was starting to worry there wouldn't be any left for you."

"Everyone gets his fair share," said Jenda Schleim. "And don't forget to save some for Albie's trip."

"Where is he going?" said Tony.

"We'll tell you later," Ernie said, smacking his lips.

Tony found it odd. Not that Ernie had ever been the type to insist on manners, but he didn't usually smack his lips.

In general, considering the cramped living conditions, table manners in the ghetto weren't all that bad. Few people ate with a knife and fork, but then again, few people ate only with their hands. Most of the ghetto's inhabitants used a spoon for all their meals. If there had been chicken, it goes without saying, they would have picked it apart with their fingers. But there wasn't any. Whatever the boys were eating, though, it was something like chicken. At least it looked that way to Tony.

"What is that?" he asked his mother.

"We'll tell you that later too," said Ernie.

Tony took a piece.

It tasted good. But that didn't necessarily mean anything. In the ghetto, almost everything tasted good. There may have been people who, as noted earlier, for religious reasons refused to eat ground meat, but if they had eaten it, they would have thought it tasted good.

Still, Tony couldn't figure out for the life of him what it was. And he was something of an expert. He could tell whether a dumpling had been prepared in the kitchen of Q 206, the Hannover Barracks, or the Magdeburg Barracks. He could even tell which cook had made it. He could taste the difference between the potato soup from the Ústí nad Labem Barracks and the potato soup from the Jugendheim at a distance of five feet, just from the smell. And if he couldn't, it was only because they had gotten some new seasoning in the kitchen. But no matter how hard he tried, he couldn't identify the food he was eating now. He got so absorbed in trying to figure it out, for a while he forgot why he had come there in the first place.

It was sad, but understandable. Man is a reed blowing in the wind. And meat this tasty, in these circumstances, was like a strong wind, if not an outright gale. In fact, you might say it testifies to the unusual strength of Tony's character that he only swallowed a few mouthfuls before asking where the dog was. Nobody there seemed too interested. It was almost as if they were trying to gloss over it.

"First get your belly full, then we'll explain," said Jenda. He ate with great gusto, if not quite as eagerly as Ledecký. Partly because he did everything differently from Ledecký, and partly because, as he put it, "You can't afford to overeat if you want to be in theater. At least not when you're young. Once you start playing character roles, that's something different."

"Just go ahead and eat, Tony," said Nurse Lili.

She sat next to Jenda Schleim, her hair streaked with grease from her constant fiddling with it. Tony thought she seemed kind of drunk. Not that he was the best judge. He'd never actually seen anyone truly drunk. But sometimes people seemed drunk to him even when they hadn't had a drop to drink. Maybe, he thought, it's because they're in such a good mood that if they had something to drink, they would get drunk. But there wasn't, so they just seemed that way. If there had been something to drink, though, they would definitely have been drunk.

"This is delicious," said Ledecký. "Reminds me of pigeon, or rabbit."

"Excuse me?" said Jenda Schleim. "Pigeon tastes nothing like rabbit."

"What does it remind you of, Albie?" Tony's mother asked.

"Bullshit," Albie said. He was in a foul mood. Clearly he wasn't too pleased to be going away.

Still, that aside, it had to be said, Jenda was right: Pigeon tastes substantially different from rabbit. In Ledecký's defense, though, it ought to be pointed out that it had been a long time since he'd eaten either one. Ration cards for poultry and pork were the first ones the Germans had taken away from the Jews. Poultry was a luxury food, according to the Germans, and no God-fearing Jew would eat pork anyway. The godless ones could either get used to it or become religious, in which case they wouldn't miss it. Little by little, all their other ration cards were taken away as well, so that rations in the ghetto were actually more or less the same as rations for Jews living in Prague and other places.

The difference, of course, was that the ghetto had no black market.

Many inhabitants of the ghetto, especially those who were less affluent, hadn't been able to afford goods on the black market before they came here anyway, so being in the ghetto didn't actually seem so much worse. The food here was basically the same, and at least as Jews they weren't banned from public transportation— even though there was no public transportation, what did they need it for anyway? you could cross the ghetto on foot in five minutes, it was actually pretty nice—and there were plenty of theater and music performances, which they weren't allowed to attend in Prague and other towns. Of course there were also transports to the camps from here, the same as in Prague and elsewhere. The only thing really unpleasant was that the only other people you had contact with was Jews. But given that everywhere else in the country Jews were forced to wear stars and weren't allowed to associate with Aryans, that wasn't so much of a difference either.

Tony finished eating and wiped his hands with a napkin.

"Tasty, huh?" said Ledecký.

"Yes," said Tony. "Very."

"In that case, we can tell you now."

"What?"

"The meat came from Fifi," said Ledecký. "But don't worry. I felt bad at first too. But then it tasted so good."

As if to reinforce his words, he reached into the bowl for another thigh.

"Come on now," said Jenda. "You don't have to wolf it all down yourself."

"It's only my third serving," Ledecký said. He lifted the thigh to his mouth and took a bite. He didn't look like he felt the slightest bit of guilt. Toward Jenda or toward Fifi.

"I don't feel guilty," Tony said. "But I don't understand. Who's Fifi?" Even as he said it, though, he already had a hunch.

"Fifi is, or rather was, the SS-Sturmbannführer's dog," said Jenda. "His ratter, to be precise."

He briefly described how they had set out in search of little Fifi with the good intention of taking her in and caring for her, but they had been foiled by the fact that the little monster barked so loud it woke up the SS-Sturmbannführer, since it was nighttime and he was asleep, so they had been forced, as much as it pained them, to wrap their hands around the little beast's tiny throat, and, well, the next thing you know . . .

"So you strangled her," said Tony, feeling a knot in his stomach.

"Absolutely not," said Jenda. "Nobody here would be stuffing their face with Fifi if we had strangled her. That would be sick. We stabbed her, in accordance with all the rules. Then we divided her up. Liza oversaw the whole thing. We got three servings each. You still have one left."

"I don't want anymore," said Tony. "We were going to protect her."

"Are you kidding?" said Jenda. "How were we supposed to protect her when she was trying to bite me? She was the most spoiled dog I've ever seen. I bet she wouldn't even have let us protect her. She had it cushy with the SS-Sturmbannführer. They even gave her spinach, I heard."

"Could be," said Ledecký, taking a bite of the thigh. "Dogs from ritzy families tend to live pretty well. We used to have a Doberman named Alfred." He usually didn't talk much about his aristocratic past, but he proceeded to describe at length every dog his family had ever owned. From the greyhound that had belonged to the mistress of his grandfather, Ledecký von Ullenstein, to the little mutt that belonged to the gatekeeper Nováček at the castle in Vratimovice, where Freiherr SS Obergruppenführer Buchholz now resided.

He clearly relished the thought.

But Tony wasn't really listening. He was sad. Even though he had originally assumed the ratter would have a different name (Buddy or Alfred), he still felt sorry for Fifi. Maybe even more than he would have otherwise.

"Fifi," it sounded so helpless. At least a Buddy or an Alfred would have bitten Jenda on the hand. But Fifi was too weak.

"She isn't exactly beefy," Tony's mother commented.

"There's plenty of meat on her, for a ratter," Ernie said. "Hey, Ledecký, just make sure you don't overdo it. I hear food poisoning from dog meat is the worst."

"I'm sure little Fifi isn't poisonous," said Ledecký, licking his lips. "She was a friendly dog."

If only Fifi wasn't a little ratter, thought Tony. If only she'd been a sheepdog, or a German shepherd. Supposedly some dogs are trained to tear people to pieces.

"Dog is a man's best friend," said Ernie. "I think that's from the Bible."

"Nope," said Ledecký. "It's not the Bible or the Talmud. Plus it depends what kind of man. Little Fifi, as I'm sure you realize, was the Sturmbannführer's friend, or girlfriend. And the Sturmbannführer was definitely not our friend."

"It still seems uncivilized," Ernie said.

"By the way," said Jenda Schleim, "people eat dog's meat in Shakespeare."

"Could be," said Ledecký. "But if you're trying to tell me Hamlet ate a ratter when he broke up with Ophelia, because he was so heartbroken, I don't believe you."

"You have no idea what theater is," said Jenda

Schleim, adopting an offended tone. "I would even go so far as to call you atheatrical."

"Knock it off, you two," said Ernie. "Who are we trying to kid? Fifi could still be here right now if we'd only been more patient. We wanted to start a society for the prevention of cruelty to animals, and the first ratter we run into, instead of protecting it, we kill it."

"Well, what were we supposed to do?" said Jenda. "I couldn't find any other meat. You didn't bring any either. And we couldn't go without a party, could we? I don't know what you're getting so upset about all of a sudden."

"I'm not upset," said Ernie. "I'm just saying we shouldn't exactly be proud of ourselves. Not to mention, it looks the kid here is going to start bawling on us any second."

"I'm not bawling," said Tony. But he could feel the tears running down his face.

"No reason to," said Ledecký. "Just make sure you wipe your eyes. You're likely to end up with an inflammation otherwise. That's what happens to people around here who cry."

Tony wiped his eyes with his sleeve. He didn't want to take out his handkerchief. It would have looked silly. And besides, it was all greasy from Fifi.

"Every animal lover makes a blunder once in a while," Ledecký consoled him. "I'll bet even the lady in charge of the SPCA sometimes steps on a worm."

"I'm sure," Tony said. He even smiled a little. "So are you saying an earthworm's an animal? Maybe we could protect worms then. There are plenty of them around here."

"I don't know what we're going to do," said Ledecký in a dejected voice. He turned back to licking his bowl.

But there was still one more bowl left. And it was full.

Tony saw it and felt bad about Fifi all over again. "I don't understand," he said to Jenda. "Before, you said you had to do it because the Sturmbannführer was there, and now you're saying you did it because you needed the meat for our party. So was he there, or wasn't he?"

"He wasn't there," said Jenda Schleim. "But he could have come."

Needless to say, that didn't satisfy Tony. He knew that line of reasoning all too well from Mr. Abeles and Mr. Löwy. For example, the sun would be shining, but Mr. Löwy would ask someone to bring his trench coat. "It's shining now," he would say, "but it might rain. Not only that, but it might rain lemons from the sky. That might happen too, for all we know. There are things that can happen and things that can't. But sometimes it happens that what can't happen does. And even if it doesn't happen, something else might."

Tony didn't fall for it. "So that's why you did 'it'?"

"I'll tell you how it was," said Jenda. "We really had to do 'it.' But the thing is, we really wanted to do 'it.' See? Because we found out that Albie here got this nicely typed piece of paper saying to report to such and such a place at such and such a time . . ."

"It was a summons for the transport," Tony's mother said.

"Which is a pretty serious thing, I think you'd agree," said Jenda. "Serious enough that we felt like we needed to throw a farewell feast for Albie. Which meant we had to do 'it' to Fifi."

"But you didn't have to," Tony said. He didn't like being lectured to. He knew about serious things. Once, back when they were still living in Prague, he'd had tickets to go see a Laurel and Hardy movie when his mother came and told him something serious had happened: His uncle Harry had died. Another time he'd had to leave a soccer match at halftime, with the Kleiderkammer leading 2–1, when old lady Poláková broke her arm. Now something serious had happened again. Albie Feld had been assigned to a transport. So they decided to eat Fifi. Tony vehemently disagreed. It didn't seem right to him.

"So there you have it," said Albie. "Now you know the whole story. Have another piece of meat."

Tony replied in a voice so soft you could barely hear it. "No, thank you," he said. "I've lost my appetite."

He couldn't bring himself to eat Fifi. He would have spent the rest of his life thinking of Buddy or Alfred.

"So where are you are going, anyway?" Jenda asked Albie.

"Destination unknown," Albie answered bitterly.

I suppose he would rather go someplace he knows, Tony thought. He too would have preferred going to Hamr nad Jezerem, where they used to go camping every year, than Dobřichovice, for example, where he had never been.

"Wherever you go," said Jenda, "there will be some kind of theater there. There's theater everywhere. That's my theory."

"That's a dumb theory," said Ledecký. "There isn't any theater at the North Pole."

"That's because there are no people there, just polar bears," Jenda said. "And they're about as atheatrical as you are. But just in case there isn't any theater up in Poland, just think about me two weeks from today. I'll be making my premiere as Khlestakov."

"Don't worry about me, boys," said Albie. "I'll get by."

He'll get by, Tony thought. Everybody needs a goalkeeper. It wasn't like forwards, or any of the other positions in which he had excelled on the little pitch in the yard of Hannover Barracks. Forwards are a dime a dozen. They might not be any good on a regulation field. But a goalie, that's different. Goalies are always in demand.

"So you don't think it's worth appealing?" Ledecký said. "I'm sure you've got lots of friends in Magdeburg Barracks."[7]

"No, not anymore," said Albie. "But come on, guys. Stop acting like it's my funeral. I'm sorry I have to leave too. But do you see me crying? No. This was like home to me. I built this place. But what're you going to do? I'll miss every one of you," he said, giving Lili and Liza a pat on the rear end. "But I'm not going to cry."

In recognition of the moment's solemnity, neither of the women squealed.

"How about a farewell go with the ladies?" said Jenda.

"No," said Albie. "I don't want to tire myself out before the trip."

---

7) Magdeburg Barracks housed the Ältestenrat, or Jewish Council of Elders. See note 3, above.

From there, the conversation moved on to the usual range of topics.

Jenda Schleim decided he would try one more time to convince Tony to take another piece of Fifi. "Why not?" he kidded. "Go ahead. The only thing you aren't allowed to eat now is worms."

So Tony took a piece.

Later he felt a little ashamed, but he said it tasted pretty normal. Like a pretty normal dog.

CHAPTER 5

IN WHICH WE LEARN ABOUT THE MYSTERIOUS
BOX AND, EVENTUALLY, WHAT'S IN IT

Tony ate too much Fifi. It gave him stomach problems for several days afterward. He even threw up, which in the ghetto was seen as a luxury.

But his old appetite soon returned.

The old men called it hunger. But it was mainly a question of terminology. Tony had never experienced hunger. The young people in the ghetto received bigger rations, and supplemented them in all sorts of ways. Tony's mother, for instance, brought him a dumpling from the kitchen every week. She often apologized for not bringing more. "It was all I could find," she would say. Lately, though, she had also been bringing a quarter loaf of bread.

After Albie's departure, she didn't pair off with any of the other boys, instead taking up with bald Eddie Spitz, from the bakery. Tony didn't like him. He may have been nice enough, but he was too staid for his mother as far as Tony was concerned. Tony gave him credit for stealing bread from the bakery, but it wasn't that big a deal. Everyone who could, stole in the ghetto.

It put Tony in a grouchy mood. Not only that, but ever since Albie had left, he was bored.

There were no more soccer matches. The men bickered less than they used to. Mr. Kohn, from the Engineers' Barracks, no longer visited Mr. Löwy to swap books with him. Ernie was impossible to get hold of. (Tony went by the attic several times, but never found him there.)

So he was glad when at least Ledecký stopped in for a visit.

He was lugging a large white box with him.

It wasn't actually white so much as yellow, like discolored teeth, but given conditions in the ghetto it was relatively white.

"What's in there?" Tony asked right away.

"Just a minute before I skin it," Ledecký replied, making himself comfortable on the bed.

Tony didn't like it when people put him off with sayings or proverbs, so he didn't follow up, but he couldn't take his eyes off the box.

Ledecký set the box down next to him on the mattress.

That awoke the ire of Mr. Glaser and Sons.

"No foreign objects on the bed. It isn't hygienic."

"This box is probably cleaner than I am," Ledecký said.

"You shouldn't be sitting on the bed either," said Mr. Glaser and Sons. "If Nurse Maria Louisa were here, she would show you."

"But Nurse Anna is on duty today," Tony said.

"That's no guarantee that Nurse Maria Louisa won't stop in," said Mr. Glaser and Sons. "The head nurse could come too."

The conversation turned to order. How some people don't know how to maintain it.

Meanwhile Tony pressed Ledecký to reveal what was inside the box.

But Ledecký refused to say. "There are some more important matters we have to take care of first," he said, pulling a dumpling wrapped in paper out of his pocket. "This is for you from Ernie."

"Thank you," Tony said. He took a bite of the dumpling. It wasn't the freshest he'd ever tasted, but it wasn't bad.

"Is there somewhere I can throw away this piece of paper?" Ledecký asked. Clearly he was trying to prove to Mr. Glaser and Sons that he had a sense of order.

Mr. Glaser and Sons noted his gesture with satisfaction. "The wastebasket," he said. "It's out in the hallway. We don't need one in here. After all, how much garbage can six people make?"

He was right. Not much was thrown away in the ghetto. Professor Steinbach threw away the skins from the potatoes he peeled. But it wasn't enough for them to need their own wastebasket.

When Tony was finished eating the dumpling, Ledecký, somewhat nonsensically, said, "Ernie said to ask if you were hungry."

"No," said Tony. "I've got everything I need."

"Liza's still bringing you bread?" asked Ledecký.

"Yep," said Tony. "She's going out with Eddie Spitz now, you know."

"So you've got plenty of bread."

"Yep," said Tony.

As he said it, though, he made a face to indicate he wasn't too enthused about his mother's bald-headed boyfriend. Then he said something to that effect.

Ledecký disagreed. "Eddie Spitz, I'll have you know, is a fine man. I know you were used to Albie. But seriously, Eddie is a good guy."

"Maybe," said Tony. "But I doubt I'll ever get used to him. I know myself. I get used to things fast. I got used to Jenda Schleim in two days. Albie took a week. And it wasn't even a day for Ernie."

"Nothing you can do about it," Ledecký said. "So what about your animals? You still planning to start that club?"

"Of course. I think about it constantly."

That wasn't entirely true. Lately he hadn't been giving it as much thought as he used to. He was feeling kind of discouraged. And whenever he felt sick to his stomach, he forbade himself from even so much as thinking about animals. He couldn't afford to. But he was glad he didn't have to talk about Eddie Spitz anymore.

"So you still want to protect worms?" Ledecký asked.

"No," said Tony. "The more I think about it, the more I feel like worms wouldn't make sense. It wouldn't be right for big kids like you and Ernie and Jenda. Protecting worms is more a job for little boys. My idea was everyone should choose whatever animal they like best."

"You may be on to something," said Ledecký. "Ernie could be in charge of canaries. He told me one time he used to have a canary at home named Petey."

He paused and thought a moment.

"The only problem is, as far as I know, there are no canaries in the ghetto. If there were, I would know about it."

Mr. Glaser and Sons objected. "How could you know?" he said. "Nobody in the ghetto knows anything for sure. Nobody even knows what will happen to them tomorrow, so how could they know whether there are canaries in the ghetto or not?"

Ledecký said it wasn't about which animals were in the ghetto and which animals weren't, but who was

going to protect what. "I could do horses," he said. "I took riding lessons, back in the day. I might even be able to teach the boys."

Mr. Löwy pointed out that, as a member of the society for the prevention of cruelty to animals, he wouldn't be allowed to use spurs.

"That goes without saying," Ledecký said.

"Some beasts you can't even control with a whip, never mind spurs," said Mr. Löwy.

But Ledecký said he could handle his horse just fine without spurs or a whip. "Why would I do that when it would get me expelled from our society?" he said. "It wouldn't be worth the risk, right, Tony?" Then he said maybe Jenda Schleim should be in charge of bears. "A bear is a theatrical animal, after all. There's even a bear in *The Bartered Bride*."

When Mr. Löwy objected that the bear in *The Bartered Bride* wasn't really a bear but Vašek, the wealthy landowner's son, Ledecký said that didn't matter, since everyone initially thought it was a bear. He had thought so too at first, so you could say there was a bear in *The Bartered Bride*, since even though it wasn't one, there was.

Mr. Löwy was so confused by Ledecký's argument that he conceded.

Then they all agreed that Tony would be in charge of protecting dogs. "Even if you did eat Fifi in the end,"

Ledecký said. "You've got the best relationship with dogs of any boy in camp. That's obvious from how long you hesitated before you took a bite. And even then, you didn't enjoy it as much as everyone else."

"No, I didn't," Tony said with a slight grimace. His stomach still wasn't completely back to normal.

Then he turned his attention back to the mysterious box. I wonder what could be in it, he thought. He could hear a rattling sound from inside. It also struck Tony as suspicious that Ledecký had brought up the SPCA so out of the blue like that. But he didn't want to ask him straight out. Not when he was making such a fuss about the whole thing.

Meanwhile the men were also getting curious.

"I used to sell margarine in boxes like that," said Mr. Löwy. "Sana. Or was it Vitelo?"

"So you didn't carry butter," Mr. Glaser and Sons said scornfully.

"I kept the butter in the fridge," Mr. Löwy said.

Mr. Brisch began examining the box. "For zat boks," he said, "you vill not get more zan two ghetto marks."[8] He didn't think it was worth very much, apparently.

---

8) In the ghetto, there was a saying that the Germans gave the Jews two great gifts: their own police (the Ghettowache) and their own currency (Ghetto-Geld). The Ghettowache didn't protect anyone, and Ghetto-Geld didn't buy you anything.

But Ledecký was undeterred. "It isn't the box. It's what's inside. Take a guess, Tony."

"It's something alive."

"Bingo. But what?"

"A worm," Tony said.

"Yuck," said Ledecký. "That's some imagination you've got. Do you really think I would bring you a worm to the hospital?"

"Then some kind of bug," Tony said. He sounded disappointed. He didn't much like bugs. Besides, he could catch a roach or earwig any time he wanted. Even in L 315.

"No, not a bug," said Mr. Löwy. "It must be something bigger. Maybe a small dog."

"No," said Ledecký. "Not that. Our experience with small dogs hasn't been very good, has it, Tony?"

"No, it hasn't," Tony said glumly. He remembered again how bad he had felt about Fifi.

"Vot about little lizard?" Mr. Brisch said. "Vhen ve vere little boy, ve catch zem all ze time."

"Nope," said Ledecký. "Not a lizard either."

"A squirrel?" Tony asked.

"Are you kidding?" Ledecký said. "You know how big the box would have to be? Have you ever seen a squirrel?"

"Sure," said Tony. "But I don't really remember it."

"Maybe it's a frog," said Mr. Löwy. "When we were boys, we used to go catch frogs down at the pond."

"Please," said Mr. Glaser and Sons. "Do you see any pond here? There isn't a pond for miles around. The only part of this country with ponds is southern Bohemia."

"Some frogs can live in puddles," Mr. Löwy said. "Don't you remember the ditty? *See the puddle in the street / See the toad crawl at your feet.*"

"That's just poetic license," said Mr. Glaser and Sons. "Frogs don't actually live in puddles. And if they did, then they couldn't survive in a box."

"All right then, I give up," Tony said. He couldn't stand it anymore.

Ledecký lifted the lid just enough for him to peek inside.

"A mouse," Tony said. "That's fantastic."

He could have whooped for joy. But he voiced his happiness quietly. Tony was experienced for a boy of thirteen, and he had a hunch not everyone would be so excited about his mouse. Some of them might even turn their noses up at it.

That became obvious right away.

"A mouse," said Mr. Glaser and Sons. "That doesn't strike me as too suitable an animal for a hospital."

"It's certainly better than a worm," said Mr. Löwy.

"Who knows where a worm might crawl? Whereas a mouse you can keep an eye on. Especially if it's in a box."

Even Mr. Brisch, who Tony had expected to back him up, had reservations. "I haff nussink against ze mouse," he said. "But I sink ze white mouse is better, no? For ze hospital? Here is everysink white: ze nurse outfit, ze valls, even ze bed."

"Actually, I'd say everything here is gray, just like the mouse," Ledecký countered.

"Because it no vash," said Mr. Brisch. "But in ze hospital it should be everysink vhite."

"By the way," said Mr. Glaser and Sons, "that wall wasn't white, it was blue. And nobody ever washed it. Who ever heard of washing a wall?"

Tony took advantage of the momentary discord between the two men to ask Ledecký how to handle the mouse, how to feed it, and what its name was.

Ledecký told him the mouse was called Helga, that he needed to handle it with care, and that it ate everything, even paper.

"Well, we've got plenty of that," said Tony. "I could even take some from the toilets."

But seeing that the two men were still grousing at each other, he decided to call for Nurse Anna. She came right away.

But when Tony showed her the box with Helga in it, she squealed in fear. Then, when he tried to convince her that Helga was totally harmless by letting her out of the box, neglecting the fact that Mr. Adamson was right in the middle of his afternoon prayer, Nurse Anna leaped onto Mr. Adamson's bed and wouldn't come down until Tony had deposited Helga back in the box and Mr. Adamson had finished praying.

Once she was back on solid ground (i.e., the floor), she maintained a firmly negative stance. She said she didn't see how anyone could think it was a good idea to bring a mouse into a hospital.

"I just wanted Tony to have something to remember us by," said Ledecký. "Seeing as we ate Fifi."

"What do you mean, remember you by?"

Ledecký paused hesitantly. "We've been summoned for the transport. Me and Jenda Schleim."

"Oh, I see," said Nurse Anna.

Even she couldn't help but be affected.

Lately there had been one transport after the next, so everyone in the ghetto was used to it by now, but still, anyone who was going away on a transport was respected, to a degree. It didn't earn them any special sympathy or privileges, but on the other hand, you couldn't really chastise them for bringing their friend in the hospital a mouse.

So Nurse Anna just straightened out the comforter on Mr. Adamson's bed (she had trampled all over it), glanced at the thermometer, and walked out again.

Which amounted to her giving approval for Helga to be in the room.

Everyone's attention turned from Helga to Ledecký.

"When ze departure?" asked Mr. Brisch.

"Tomorrow," said Ledecký. "I have number Ec 346."

"That's interesting," said Tony. "Albie had En 346."

"Maybe," Ledecký said. "But Ec 346 is better. It's easier to remember. Like the electric company."

"Right," said Tony. "Still, it's strange you're leaving. I always thought you were protected."

"I was. But the fact that my great-great-grandfather fought on the side of the Habsburgs at White Mountain doesn't do me any good anymore. Last year it still helped. This year, no."

"That's a shame," said Tony.

He asked Ledecký how many pieces of luggage he was taking with him.

"One," said Ledecký. "And a rucksack on my back."

"Hm," said Tony. "That isn't much."

"It's plenty," said Ledecký. "For the couple of shirts and pants I've got."

"For your clothes it is, yeah, but I had something else in mind."

"What's that?"

"I was wondering if you'd mind taking some oats along with you," said Tony. "You know, in case there are any horses where you're going. But if all you've got is one suitcase . . ."

"I'll think about it," said Ledecký.

But from the way he was smiling, Tony could tell that he wouldn't do it.

Actually, Tony's idea of bringing a suitcase full of oats wasn't as silly as it might have seemed. Plenty of so-called sensible adults in the ghetto had considered not bringing anything with them, rather than bring something only to have the Germans take it away. Why not oats?

Otherwise, for the most part, people took warm clothes. A few were convinced the transports were headed for warmer climes. Ethiopia, say, or Liberia. But even they didn't neglect to bring a pair or two of warm underwear and some sweaters. If it got too hot, they could always take them off.

Ledecký said good-bye to Tony. He made him promise to be careful and keep an eye on his mother.

"I'll try," Tony said.

He didn't have any illusions, though. His mother wasn't the type to take advice, especially not from her son. At one point, he had made some comments about her involvement with Jenda Schleim. She didn't look kindly on it. "I'm the adult here," she had said. So Tony, the child, decided to keep his mouth shut. Shortly after that, his mother had started going around with Albie Feld, so he no longer had any reason to complain. Now she was going around with someone he disliked even more than Jenda. But he didn't have any reason to think it would turn out any better than last time, if he tried to talk her out of it. His mother was a stubborn woman. How many times had she said now, "Do I tell you what to do with your animals?" He found it extremely annoying. Especially now that he had the mouse. He was going to have enough trouble with Helga as it is.

It was her first time in the hospital in her life, and she didn't know how things were run. She had no idea how to act.

But Tony was confident that eventually he would teach her.

CHAPTER 6

IN WHICH WE LEARN ABOUT ERNIE'S PLAN

The next day, Tony woke up early. It wasn't even fully light yet.

He wanted to check in on Helga, but as he leaned out of his bed to look, he nearly woke Mr. Glaser and Sons, so instead he decided to pretend he was going to the toilet. On the way, though, he ran into Nurse Maria Louisa, who was alarmed to see him going to the toilet in light pajamas, so she ordered him to go back and put on his flannel ones, and said she would be right back to check and make sure he had done as she asked.

So even when Tony returned from the toilet, he didn't open Helga's box.

On top of that, right after reveille, Mr. Glaser and Sons announced that he hadn't slept a wink all night because "that animal" had been making such a terrible racket.

Mr. Löwy asked him, sarcastically, how it was then that Nurse Maria Louisa hadn't been able to wake him up, but Mr. Glaser and Sons claimed that he had fainted, which happened to him when he couldn't sleep, like a sort of coma.

Mr. Löwy pointed out that he was snoring pretty loudly for someone in a coma, but it was no use. The benevolence with which the men had received Helga the day before had been disrupted, and when Tony let Helga out of the box, even the normally tolerant Professor Steinbach remarked that it wasn't appropriate to let her out while Mr. Adamson was praying.

Mr. Brisch replied, aptly, that Mr. Adamson prayed all the time, so if it depended on him, the mouse would have to stay locked up inside the box forever, slowly degenerating, the same as people do when they don't get out of bed, let alone take a walk around the ghetto every once in a while. But his words had no effect on the attitude of the room's occupants toward Helga. If anything, just the opposite. Tony noticed that even Mr. Brisch shuddered when Helga ran across his hand.

Mr. Glaser and Sons categorically forbade Helga to enter the area around his bed.

Even when Ernie showed up, the men didn't welcome him warmly.

"This is a hospital, not a birdhouse!" said Mr. Glaser and Sons. "First you bring in a mouse, now a friend. What is it going to be next?"

Mr. Löwy objected that surely there was a difference between a mouse and a boy's friend. And Mr. Brisch chimed in that comparing a human to an animal was fascism.

"Do you mean to imply that I'm a fascist?" asked Mr. Glaser and Sons.

Nevertheless, Ernie seemed not to notice any of it. He didn't even tell the men hello, instead starting right in angrily describing to Tony how Jenda Schleim and Ledecký had gone away. Mr. Glaser and Sons interrupted to ask how heavy their bags had been, and Ernie barked back that he ought to know you can only take sixty-five pounds, at which Mr. Glaser and Sons took offense, since of course he knew, but he was just curious whether or not the Germans had made an exception this time. After all, they could have ordered them to take ninety pounds on this transport, or forty-five. "The Germans get all kinds of ideas, what do we know?" he said.

Tony wanted to keep the dispute from escalating, so he offered to show Helga to Ernie.

But Ernie acted insulted, saying all Tony cared about was his mouse now; he wasn't thinking of his friends anymore. "They're out there and here you are, making a fuss over some mouse."

"I'm not making a fuss," Tony said. "Besides, I'll have you know, I've been thinking of them, a lot. Just yesterday I was wondering if I should remind Jenda that he's in charge of bears. Just in case he runs into one. I hear there are lots of them in the Carpathians."

"I vonder if ze bears are running avay from ze front," said Mr. Brisch.

But Ernie wasn't in the mood to talk about bears.

"If you'd seen those cattle cars they put them in," he said, "you wouldn't be worrying about bears. They were packed in there like herrings."

"Are herrings and sardines the same thing or different?" Tony wondered.

"I don't know," said Ernie. "But I couldn't care less right now. I've got other problems."

"Like what?"

"I'm not riding out of here on that cattle car. I made up my mind."

"Good for you," said Tony. "I hear they're really uncomfortable. So how are you going then?"

It turned out Ernie didn't just mean he objected to cattle cars as a form of transportation. He didn't intend to leave the ghetto, period, by any means.

"I'm not going anywhere," he said. "I'd rather make a run for it over the ramparts."

Terezín was an old eighteenth-century fortress town, so by that, he meant escape.

"It's also a matter of honor," said Ernie. He was a former boy scout.

Tony had to admit, his friend had a point. Even if no one dared ask it of them, for the sake of the ghetto inhabitants' future, it was good for someone to protest every once in a while. Escaping wasn't the only way to protest of course, as Mr. Löwy explained. A man by the name of

Karl Weiss, from Vienna, had decided to protest the low food rations for older people by staging a hunger strike. Within a week, he nearly died. But given that a hundred and sixty other people died in the ghetto during that week who weren't on hunger strike, nobody noticed. "Then again," Mr. Glaser and Sons said, "Mr. Fantl, from Vinohrady in Prague, walked back and forth in front of the Magdeburg Barracks shouting that Hitler was a jerk. Since there weren't any Germans in hearing range at the time, the Council of Elders quickly called a meeting and decided to toss him in the Ghettogefängnis.[9] Mr. Fantl just went on shouting, so they transferred him to the psychiatric unit. Once he got there he stopped, since the other patients didn't take him seriously."

But even though Tony knew all these stories, he still admired Ernie.

"You always were the bravest of all the boys," he said.

"Nah," said Ernie. "Anyone would do the same. They just didn't think of it."

"Maybe," said Tony. But maybe not, he thought. Ledecký had always been in favor of order on principle.

---

9) The Ghettogefängnis, unlike the jail in headquarters, was guarded only by Jews from the Ghettowache, so it wasn't really a jail. The prisoners there spent most of their time playing cards. If you didn't know how to play rummy, you would end up pretty bored.

And Albie Feld, the one time they had talked about making an escape, had said he wouldn't be able to do it because he stood out too much.

Which was true, but on the other hand, Ernie had red hair and freckles. And he wasn't making any excuses.

"You're practically a hero," Tony said.

"No, not me. I just think someone's got to do something."

"I want to do something too," said Tony. "That's why I want to start the SPCA. And now I've got Helga."

"That's just a game," said Ernie.

"Everysink is game," said Mr. Brisch. "Vhere ends life and vhere begins game? Don't esk me. Zis vhat is doink ze little man mit ze mustache and ze hair, it is also game. But it effects ze life. Ozervise I agree vith you. Vhot ve need is actif resistance. Only zat vill impress ze Germans."

"So why don't you do something active?" said Mr. Glaser and Sons. He didn't like theory. He was a practical man.

"Who says I am not?" said Mr. Brisch. "I maybe do somesink you do not know."

It was entirely possible that he was doing something Mr. Glaser and Sons didn't know about. He did go out on his own every Sunday, after all. Before Tony had gotten to know Mr. Brisch better, he had even suspected him of meeting in secret with some men who were forging a secret plot. What kind of plot he had no idea, but he imagined they were scheming to blow up the Magdeburg Barracks. Mr. Brisch complained about the barracks a lot.

One time Tony had shared his suspicions with Mr. Löwy, but Mr. Löwy had said it was more likely Mr. Brisch was going to visit his wife. Tony knew for a fact that he wasn't, though, since for the past two months she had been seeing the little man who inspected the meat at the butcher's shop.

Naturally he couldn't say so to Mr. Löwy, so instead he just pretended he was going on a walk. Maybe while he walked he was thinking about his former wife or imagining the new world order. Tony wasn't sure. But either way, he thought highly of Mr. Brisch.

"Mr. Brisch is a Communist," Tony told Ernie.

"Yeah," Ernie said absently. "I thought so. But I don't have time for talk now."

"Communist is no talk," said Mr. Brisch. "Communist is act. So I praise you. Escape, that is act."

"I approve too," Tony said. He had the feeling Ernie was still bothered by what had happened with Fifi, so he added, "I'm not mad at you about Fifi, you know that, right? I've got Helga now, and besides, I think it

really helped Albie. At least he went to the transport with a good meal in his belly. Cooking Fifi was the right thing to do."

"I don't know," said Ernie. "In my opinion, people shouldn't eat dogs. I was opposed."

"What do you mean, 'opposed'?" Tony said. "I thought you all decided on it when you found out Albie was going on the transport."

"That's where blind passion will lead you," said Ernie. "It was decided long before that. Jenda Schleim just made that up so you wouldn't feel so bad."

He stopped and reflected on Jenda's fate.

"Poor guy. He was looking forward so much to playing Khlastakov."

"Khlestakov," Tony corrected him, remembering the name of the character in the play. He felt like bursting into tears. They shouldn't have done that to him. Nobody is that hungry. If they really wanted to eat dog that badly, they could have at least cooked up some other dog, instead of Fifi.

But he pulled himself together. "I thought you would be glad that Jenda was going away."

"Why's that?" said Ernie.

"So you could have Nurse Lili all to yourself again." Tony was referring to the fact that recently Nurse Lili had been going around with Jenda Schleim.

"Nah," Ernie said, waving his hand dismissively. "Girls aren't that important. Not one of them is worth getting in an argument with your buddy. Especially not now."

"But you guys fought over lots of other stuff."

"That's because we were buddies. You wouldn't understand."

Tony had to admit that Ernie was right. He'd gotten used to the fact that there were just things you couldn't understand when you were thirteen, no matter how you hard you tried. And if you did understand them, either you understood them wrong or you understood them but they were no use to you anyway, so you were better off just accepting that you didn't understand. But Ernie wanted to make a run for it—that much Tony understood.

He understood all too well.

"What do you think? You think I could go with you?"

"No, you're too young," Ernie said.

"It might work to your advantage, you know," Tony said. "Everybody feels sorry for kids. Even here in the ghetto, they get the biggest portions."

"Young people don't get bigger portions because they're young. They get them because they're the future of the nation," said Mr. Löwy.

"Nonsenses," said Mr. Brisch. He shot a glance at Professor Steinbach. "Chews are no nation. Nation is a German or Czechish."

"Either way," said Tony. "I just want to give this place the slip. And take Helga with me."

"You can't, Tony," said Mr. Löwy. "Look how big that box is. It would get in the way. What if they start shooting at you? How are you going to run?"

"You think?" Tony said. It hit him that he probably couldn't take Helga with him after all. She's so tiny, he thought, it wouldn't take much, just a little blow, and she would be a goner. He didn't want to risk it. Not to mention, everything indicated that Ernie wouldn't take him with him anyway.

Tony made his peace with it.

At least I'll be able to take good care of Helga, he thought.

Then Professor Steinbach decided to butt in.

Apparently he regretted not having replied to Mr. Brisch a few moments earlier.

"You'll change your mind yet, young man," he said, addressing Ernie. "What are you running from, anyway? The transports? What for? They say the transports are heading east. That's where the land of our ancestors is."

"My ancestors are from Kolín. They had a mill there," said Ernie.

But Professor Steinbach insisted. He said the ghetto was just preparation for the journey to the promised land. Poland, where the transports were headed, was the transfer station. That was why he wasn't afraid.

"So, professor, how are you going to talk with people once you get to the Holy Land?" Mr. Löwy asked.

He was referring to the fact that when Mr. Adamson, a Polish Jew from Holland who spoke only Yiddish, had first arrived in room 26, Professor Steinbach had been unable to communicate with him.

"As you know, gentlemen, I will be lecturing in Czech literature at the university in Tel Aviv," Professor Steinbach said. "Naturally, then, I will require my students to address me in Czech. It will only be to their benefit."

Tony wondered whether Professor Steinbach would be a good teacher. He probably wouldn't let his students copy off of one another during exams, but if someone didn't know the answer when he called on them in class, Tony was sure he would let them off the hook.

"But what if you need to buy something?" said Mr. Glaser and Sons. Even he was annoyed by Professor Steinbach's salon-style Zionism.

"I should hope that my standing in the academic community will be solid enough that the rector provides me with an interpreter. It could even be one of my students. Nevertheless, gentlemen, we have digressed from our topic. I was impressing upon this young man here that he ought not to act rashly."

"I've got it all figured out," said Ernie. Clearly he wasn't impressed by Professor Steinbach's argument. "I've made up my mind. And no fine words are going to stop me."

He turned to Tony and told him if he wanted to say good-bye, he should come to the ramparts the next day at two thirty.

"Ernie's amazing," Tony said once Ernie had left.

"Zat should be normal," said Mr. Brisch wistfully. "Every younk man should be rebellink. Viss your permission, chentlemen. Erlauben die Herren," he said, and took his violin out of its case.

He played for ten minutes or so. "Zat vas Mondscheinsonate by Beethoven," he said when he was finished. "Sonata for ze moonshine. But also viss a big piece of rebellion. Very big."

Tony admired the skillful movement of the older man's fingers up and down the fingerboard. He never would have guessed he was so talented. Then he turned his attention back to Helga, in the box. He had a feeling she was uneasy. It was probably the music.

Tony sat dressed in his clothes on his bed. It was pretty risky, given that Nurse Maria Louisa was on duty. In fact he was violating two hospital regulations at once: sitting up on the bed during bed-rest time and being dressed in his clothes.

Tony was impatient, though, and anyway the nurse was giving an enema to Mr. Breittfeld in room 6, so there was no danger of her coming in anytime soon. Nor was he worried that any of the other men would ring for her. They never rang. Tony appreciated that, since he was concerned that if one of them brought Helga to her attention, she would be even less understanding than Nurse Anna. As a former nun,[10] Nurse Maria Louisa had lived her whole life in the convent in

10) To be clear, Nurse Maria Louisa, although a former nun, was also a Jew under the Nuremberg Laws, like all the personnel and patients in L 315 and all the other inhabitants of the ghetto. The story was that, when the Jews began to wear yellow stars, the nuns at the convent asked if Sister Maria Louisa could be allowed not to wear one, but apparently it didn't help. Although no one knew whether she ended up having to wear one or not, now she was in the ghetto. That much was clear.

Čáslav, and she was scrupulous when it came to matters of hygiene. She definitely would have considered a mouse to be unsanitary. Even if he could prove to her that Helga was actually cleaner than, say, Mr. Adamson, he was afraid it wouldn't convince her. But the men didn't say a word.

Tony was getting impatient. "What time is it?" he asked Mr. Löwy for probably the tenth time.

"Two twenty-five p.m. Greenwich time."

"I'm supposed to be there in five minutes. And I still have to put on my sneakers," said Tony. He kept it to himself that he also wanted to pack a suitcase. Just in case. What if Ernie changed his mind and agreed to take him with him?

"If Nurse Maria Louisa wasn't on duty, I would have been there by now," he said.

It wasn't just that she would have scolded him for running away during bed rest. He could deal with that, even if Nurse Maria Louisa could give a scolding like nobody else. The problem was, she had a habit of locking the front door during bed-rest hours, so not even a mouse, literally, could get in or out of L 315 during that time. Even Helga couldn't get out, Tony thought.

"It's a catastrophe," he said out loud.

"Not yet," said Mr. Glaser and Sons. "But it might yet turn out to be. It's true, Maria Louisa is extremely

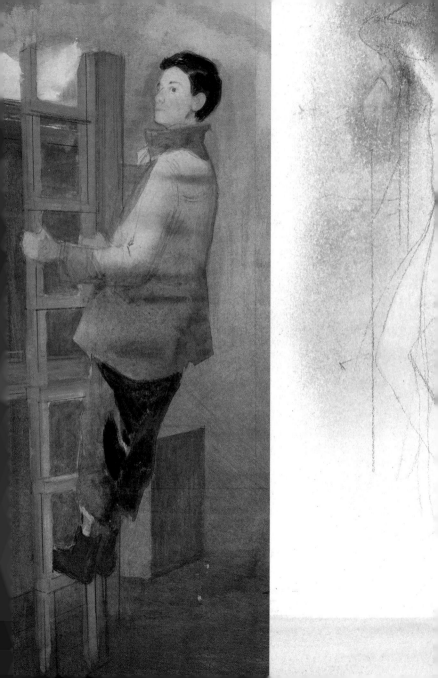

conscientious, but she might not have locked the front door. Maybe she's expecting them to bring a serious patient."

"They could just ring the bell," Mr. Löwy pointed out.

"But what if it doesn't work?" said Mr. Glaser and Sons. "This isn't a general store, Mr. Löwy. This is a hospital."

"No one should be allowed to die durink bed rest," said Mr. Brisch. "A person should only die between ten a.m. and tvelve noon. Zose are receiving hours."

Of course he was being ironic, but it didn't seem that strange to anyone. There were so many illogical regulations in the ghetto. For instance, headquarters had recently issued an order that no non-Aryans were allowed to walk their dog along the riverbank in the ghetto. The problem with that was, one, Jews weren't allowed to have a dog; two, Jews weren't allowed to walk along the riverbank; three, all Jews were required to work, so even if they were allowed to walk along the riverbank, and even if they did have a dog, they wouldn't have had the time; four, any Jew who had time couldn't have walked their dog there, since it was hard enough feeding themselves on the food rations they got, never mind feeding a dog; and five, there was no riverbank in the ghetto (there wasn't even a river). So why should the men be surprised at a regulation stating that inhabitants of the ghetto had to die between ten a.m. and twelve noon?

But Tony wasn't thinking about the theoretical consequences of Nurse Maria Louisa locking the door. Practically, it bothered him that he couldn't get out and, as a result, he might miss his chance to tell Ernie goodbye. He knew Ernie wouldn't wait. He was a stickler for punctuality. Not that he was always on time. Once, he had left Tony waiting for him over half an hour in front of the Hannover Barracks. But he always demanded it of Tony. Tony was a lot younger than him, after all.

Tony shared his concerns with Mr. Brisch, who loudly declared something had to be done.

"But what?" said Mr. Löwy. "She has the key."

"Ve vill just have to get it from her," said Mr. Brisch.

"She'll never give it to you," said Mr. Glaser and Sons. "She may have her faults, but Nurse Maria Louisa knows her duties. It's strictly forbidden for her to give the building key to patients during bed rest."

"I vill not ask it. I vill take it," said Mr. Brisch.

"Violence," said Mr. Löwy. "I don't like to see violence used against women. Especially not a former nun."

"No violence," said Mr. Brisch. "Ve use ruse of var."

There ensued a long debate about whether or not it was acceptable to use a ruse of war against Nurse Maria Louisa. Mr. Brisch argued that it was acceptable, precisely because she was a former nun and all nuns were former charges of the Jesuits. He even went so far as to claim that she would have used one against them herself. He said he had plenty of experience with nuns and men of the cloth, they were all proponents of the saying "the end justifies the means," and a ruse of war was precisely the means justified by the end, because "zat boy is goink crazies to say his friend good-bye."

Mr. Glaser and Sons objected that a man must always treat a woman with the utmost courtesy. And that a courteous man doesn't wage war on a woman, even by way of a ruse. Especially not when she's a former nun. He said for him it would be like pulling shenanigans on a rabbi's wife.

Mr. Löwy said that no one had any intention of mocking Nurse Maria Louisa; the point was to get the key. And there probably wasn't any way to get it except to deceive her. But how?

"You leafe zat to me," said Mr. Brisch, and he rang for the nurse. Apparently, she had finished with the enema in room 6, since she appeared in the doorway just seconds later.

Who knows why the men were so worried about her? She wasn't actually any more strict than the other nurses. (With the exception of Nurse Anna.) Maybe it was because she was so perfect. When she had the five o'clock shift, she would show up at five to five; when she gave an injection, you barely felt it; and nothing ever broke or spilled when she was on duty. Or maybe it was because she was so painstakingly proper. Once, when a breeze nearly blew off her cap, she dashed out of the room and wouldn't return until her hair was fully covered again. That bred respect.

"Vhat are your vishes, gentlemen?" she said. She had spent most of her life, as we already said, at the convent in Čáslav, but she still spoke Czech as badly, if not worse, than Mr. Brisch, who was from Berlin. Clearly, the Lord didn't mind.

"Geben Sie mir den Schlüssel," said Mr. Brisch. He translated to make sure Tony understood: "Gif me ze key."

By speaking in his mother tongue, he meant to demonstrate how important it was to him that Tony get the key. Mr. Brisch, as he often emphasized, had renounced his nationality. That was why he had learned Czech. "After ze var," he said, "zen ve vill see. If ze Chermans are decent people, zey vill go beck home. But if zey are ze Schweinehunde, zey vill stay here." He refused to speak the same language that Adolf Hitler used to deliver his speeches.

"Was für ein Schlüssel?" asked Nurse Maria Louisa.

"She vonders vhy ve need ze key," Mr. Brisch translated for Tony. He was happy to annoy her. As a Communist, Mr. Brisch considered clerics the enemy. You could tell he wasn't doing it solely out of conviction, but took great pleasure in it. Still, after addressing the nurse nonstop for nearly ten minutes without getting the key, it appeared that he had failed.

"She is from Chaslau und I'm from Berlin, but she is more Prussian zan I am," he whispered angrily.

"But vhat do you need ze key for?" she kept on repeating. "Ze patient does not need ze key to open ze door." She had a point. Why would a patient strapped to the bed need a key to get out? It was hard to argue with that.

Fortunately, Mr. Brisch got an idea. "We do not vant to open ze door, but ve haf made ze bet on ze key."

Mr. Löwy, picking up on his idea, jumped right in. "Mr. Brisch says it's iron, but Mr. Glaser and I say it's brass. We just want to borrow it so we can see who's right."

Tony gazed at Mr. Löwy with newfound admiration. Who knew he was such a good liar?

"He's lying through his teeth," Mr. Glaser and Sons whispered in disgust. "He picked up the habit running his grocery store. Who knows what kind of shoddy merchandise he sold."

But Nurse Maria Louisa remained doubtful.

"Und wie lange brauchen Sie den Schlüssel?" How long do you need the key for? she asked.

"Just a minute," said Mr. Brisch.

"Und Sie geben mir ihn dann gleich zurück?" And then you'll give it right back?

"Ja," said Mr. Brisch.

"Also, since you vant it so bedly," said Nurse Maria Louisa, and, shaking her head, she walked off to get the key.

When Mr. Bergmann in room 30 had a heart attack, she knew what to do; when Councilman Auersperg peed his bed, she knew what steps to take; and the day they brought a lunatic into L 315 who started acting up, she had Professor Steinbach help her tie him down, then sent him off to the psychiatrist. But when two patients made a bet to see if the building key was iron or brass? Handling that was beyond her.

Mr. Brisch gave the men their instructions. He and Tony would go to the front door. The men's assignment was to come up with some excuse (ideally, as part of the bet) to send Nurse Maria Louisa down to check on them. Then Mr. Brisch would, as he put it, "irgendwie get ze key from her."

Mr. Löwy said it wouldn't be easy to convince her to go downstairs. Partly because her duties were on the second and third floors, and partly because, as everyone knew, Nurse Maria Louisa was deeply religious, and people like that are hard to convince of anything. He knew that from his shop.

Mr. Glaser and Sons said it depended what sort of goods the shopkeeper was selling. If they were high quality, you didn't have to convince the customer much, even if they were religious. The goods sold themselves. If the product was shoddy, no one would buy it anyway.

Mr. Brisch, instead of arguing with them the way he usually did, just said he firmly believed the men would carry out their mission.

At which point the two men, surprisingly, ceased to argue, and Tony and Mr. Brisch went downstairs to the front door.

It took Mr. Brisch a while to catch his breath after walking downstairs, but then he took charge. "Hide here," he told Tony, pushing him into an alcove next to the door. "Usually a person breathes out of air vhen he goes up," he grumbled, "but vith my tuberculosis I am breazink heavy even when I am goink down." Then he shushed Tony and waited with him for Nurse Maria Louisa to come.

They had left the door upstairs open, so they could hear the men trying to persuade her. Mr. Löwy spoke louder than any of them, which surprised Tony. He hadn't realized that Mr. Löwy spoke German that well. But Nurse Maria Louisa, as expected, wouldn't budge. She never did anything unless she knew the reason why. Rumor was, she wouldn't even do what the head nurse told her to. And the head nurse wasn't exactly a nobody. Even the doctor listened to her.

The men talked and talked.

All in vain, it seemed.

Afterward, Mr. Löwy said that if she had been a barren cow he would have talked a calf out of her. Obviously, it wasn't appropriate to speak that way of a former nun, but it captured the reality of the situation. It took about fifteen minutes before Nurse Maria Louisa finally agreed to make her way downstairs.

"She vill probably change her mind," whispered Mr. Brisch to Tony. "Ladies like him, zey sink and sink over every silly sing. It's all zat classical Cherman philosophy."

Apparently, he overestimated the influence of classical German philosophy on the thinking of Nurse Maria Louisa, but she did descend the stairs unusually slowly.

"Was soll das denn heissen?" she said as she stepped off the last stair and saw Mr. Brisch by the front door.

"She esks vhat is ze meaning of zis," Mr. Brisch whispered in a triumphant tone. "But she is holding ze key." He turned to the nurse and said, in Czech: "Zat means you give ze key." It was unclear whether he'd spoken in Czech so that Tony could understand, or in order to throw her off guard. But either way, she replied, "I no give."

"Oh no?" said Mr. Brisch. "You no give? I sink you give." He tore the key from her hand and handed it off to Tony.

"Here, Tony. Now run! I keep her here."

He wrapped his arm around Nurse Maria Louisa's waist, as if to dance with her. She didn't actually know how to dance, so she shuffled and jerked as best she could, but then suddenly returned to her senses and snapped out of it.

She pushed Mr. Brisch away so hard he almost fell, and was just about to go chasing after Tony when she remembered she was on duty and wasn't allowed to leave her patients unattended. So instead, she rearranged the cap on her head, gave Mr. Brisch a withering look, and said, "Sie Schwein." You pig.

"Du Hure," you whore, Mr. Brisch replied with delight. And he bowed to her politely.

Of course he knew she wasn't a whore. But that wasn't the point right now.

Tony ran off toward the ramparts.

Even though the ghetto was small, occupying an area of barely four-tenths of a square mile, people there walked fast. No one was in a rush to get anywhere, but everyone walked fast to make it look as if they were. So running didn't make Tony conspicuous, and he was pretty fast, too. Good thing I don't have pneumothorax anymore, he thought. Otherwise I might get an embolism. He didn't actually know what an embolism was, but he remembered that before he got over his pneumothorax, Nurse Maria Louisa used to tell him, "No runnink around, Tony, or you get embolism."

He praised his sneakers in his mind. If I had heavy boots on, he thought, I wouldn't be able to run so fast. On that point, he was mistaken, however. People far weaker than him had been able to run much faster, even with heavy boots on, across the worst terrain.

He suddenly realized he had forgotten his suitcase. But he told himself it was just as well, or he wouldn't have been able to run so fast. Then he thought, Ernie's a lot more likely to take me with him if I don't have a suitcase. He knew how Ernie was. He would say, "You, I'll take. But you and the suitcase? Nothing doing. That's too much."

But then he realized he couldn't run away with Ernie anyway. He couldn't leave Helga behind. It was harder than he'd expected, taking care of her. It didn't matter if it was soft bits of napkin or hard cardboard, she wouldn't eat paper. It had to be bread. One of the men in the room would likely have to sacrifice part of his ration.

That much was clear. Tony thought he heard thunder in the distance. Wrong again. It wasn't thunder, those were gunshots.

But Tony's experience didn't extend that far. He knew the sound it made when someone got slapped in the face by an SS man. It was a little different, more distinguished somehow, than the sound of a normal slap on the face from his mother. But he'd never heard the sound of gunfire before.

As he ran up to the ramparts, he found a group of older men standing there.

They all looked very serious.

He spotted Mr. Kohn, from the Engineers' Barracks, off to one side.

"What's going on?" Tony asked him.

"They shot and killed some young boy. Supposedly he was walking along the ramparts."

"Do you know who it was?"

Mr. Kohn shrugged and threw up his hands. "Probably some very stupid Jew. If it had been a smart Jew, or even a slightly stupid Jew, he wouldn't have been walking along the ramparts in such bad weather."

Tony felt his throat go dry. It wasn't just the long run. "What if he was trying to escape?" Tony said.

"Then he was a totally stupid Jew," said Mr. Kohn. "Trying to escape now, when everyone is just trying to hang on, tooth and nail. Don't you think?"

"I don't know," said Tony. But he could feel himself getting very upset.

The last time he'd been that upset was the championship game for the ghetto soccer league. The referee had given the Cooks a penalty shot in overtime and Albie Feld caught it. He got a standing ovation. But Tony knew he'd just been lucky. He just took a guess and dove in the right direction. If Schönfeld had shot to the other side, it would have been a goal.

This time, though, whoever it was had shot to the other side. And even the best dive in the world wouldn't have made the save.

CHAPTER 8

WHICH TAKES PLACE ALMOST ENTIRELY
AT THE CEMETERY

Tony was really upset about not telling Ernie good-bye. So he made arrangements to be there for his burial, at least.

He went to see Mr. Kohn, who knew a Mr. Steiner from České Budějovice, whose brother-in-law, Karpfen, was a member of the burial crew.

At first, Karpfen refused to take Tony along with him. But once Tony told him that he didn't want any money for it, and he didn't expect to receive any special rations, Karpfen changed his mind.

"Was he a relative of yours?" Karpfen asked.

"A cousin," said Tony.

Tony gave that answer because it was more likely Karpfen would let him bury a cousin than just a friend. And to say Ernie was his brother struck him as a little bit much.

"Well, if he was your cousin, all right then," said Karpfen. "If it was somebody closer to you, I would say no. It's no use trying to bury a close relative. You get all worked up and teary-eyed, and then you can't dig properly. But as long as it's your cousin, all right."

Tony arrived at the graveyard at eight o'clock on the dot. Karpfen was already there, along with two other men. Tony was surprised. Not many people in the ghetto were so punctual about showing up for work. But then he remembered that burying someone is, after all, a more serious matter than pulling a wagon or delivering coal.

Karpfen introduced him to the other men: Dr. Neugeboren and Mr. Veselý. They greeted him rather coldly.

"A little boy like him has got no business being here," said Dr. Neugeboren. "What are we supposed to talk about, huh? When old Weinstein used to help us, he may not have done much, but at least he could tell a joke. A boy like this, though . . ."

Tony said he knew a few jokes, but Dr. Neugeboren wasn't impressed.

"There are jokes, and then there are jokes," he said. "Not every joke is suitable for the graveyard."

Mr. Veselý, who in his former life had been a stamp dealer, was concerned it would be too disturbing for Tony. "After all," he said, "burying your own cousin is no walk in the park. I never had to bury my cousin when I was that young. Come to think of it, I never buried anyone."

"I've buried people before," said Tony. He explained how right after he'd come to the ghetto, he had been assigned to the Hundertschaft. For several days (it was supposed to be a hundred, hence the name) he had not only lugged around bags full of rotten potatoes and built roads, but he had even helped out in the crematorium.

"That may be," said Mr. Veselý, "but you haven't buried a cousin yet."

"No," said Tony. "But I've carried lots of dead bodies recently."

Tony was referring to the fact that whenever someone died in L 315, he helped Nurse Anna move the deceased to another bed, so she could put new sheets on for the next patient.

Mr. Veselý was convinced.

Karpfen put on a pair of threadbare mittens, which went very nicely with his patched-up breeches, and handed out the tools.

The men weren't nearly as handy as Tony had expected. Mr. Veselý seemed to be the most dexterous of the lot, probably due to the fact that his line of work required him to use tweezers.

"Why don't we take him first, then," Karpfen suggested, gesturing with his pick to Ernie. "If it'll make the boy happy."

"You ought to be more careful with that thing," said Dr. Neugeboren. He was unnerved by the way Karpfen was swinging his pick around. "It's downright dangerous standing near you."

"Pardon me," said Karpfen, "but the worst I could do is break your glasses, and that wouldn't be so bad. You only wear them to show off, anyway."

"Excuse me, but in case you hadn't noticed, there's a boy present. Try to control yourself. At least for today."

"If you want to run with wolves, first you have to learn how to howl," Karpfen said, lifting Ernie off the ground and setting him on top of the heap.

None of the three men seemed much like wolves to Tony. In fact, they were pretty tame, he thought. If Mr. Brisch and Mr. Glaser and Sons had been burying Mr. Löwy, the arguments would have been much fiercer. But then he realized the two situations were totally different. If Mr. Brisch and Mr. Glaser and Sons had been burying Mr. Löwy, they would be burying someone they knew, whereas these men hadn't known Ernie at all.

Karpfen noticed that Tony was lost in thought. "So, what was your cousin like?" he asked.

"He was a great kid," said Tony. "He wasn't just my cousin, but my best friend, and a cook. He gave me a dumpling every day."

That was a slight exaggeration. Ernie had given him barely one dumpling a week. But he'd also given one to Tony's mother every now and then, so it wasn't exaggerating that much.

"Yes," said Dr. Neugeboren. "That's how one shows friendship in the ghetto. By giving someone a dumpling every day."

Tony could tell the doctor could have used a friend like that, who would give him a dumpling every day. Maybe even just one every other day.

"What was he thinking, trying to escape like that?" said Karpfen, grabbing Ernie by the legs and tugging him off the pile. It seemed like he was trying to place him in a position where he could better understand him.

"I don't know," said Tony.

"You ought to know," said Dr. Neugeboren, stabbing his spade into the ground. "Seeing as he gave you a dumpling every day."

"He had the most amazing ideas sometimes," said Tony. "If you can believe it, his latest idea was to set up a society for the prevention of cruelty to animals, right here in the ghetto."

"Oh, come on," said Karpfen, leaning on his pick. "Sounds kind of loopy, if you ask me."

"Not at all," said Tony. "He was just really kind-hearted. One day he saw the SS-Sturmbahnführer beating his dog, and right then and there he decided to form an SPCA."

"Uh-huh," said Karpfen.

"The dog's name was Fifi," said Tony. "He was a dachshund. Well, actually, it was a she."

"Now I get it," said Karpfen. "The SS-Sturmbahnführer wasn't feeding Fifi the way he should, so your cousin decided to find him some food fit for a dog. And there isn't much of that to be had in the ghetto, that's for sure."

"That's right," said Tony, "just like you said. Ernie couldn't stand it when someone abused an animal. And he said so. That's how come he tried to escape."

"Can't blame him," said Karpfen, staring at the hole in Ernie's forehead. "Kopfschuss, pure and simple, gents. But maybe he was already dead. Got a good ten bullets in him," he said, swinging his pick at his side.

"Watch that you don't take my head off," said Dr. Neugeboren.

"That wouldn't be such a loss," Karpfen grumbled.

"Remember, there's a boy here. Allow me to draw that to your attention yet again. And this," said Dr. Neugeboren, pointing to Ernie with his spade, "was his cousin."

"And best friend," said Mr. Veselý.

"Ernie was really super," said Tony. "Before he tried to escape, he gave me a mouse as a present. Its name is Helga."

Tony surprised himself at all the good traits he was ascribing to Ernie. But he didn't feel bad about it. I'm sure Ledecký would forgive me, he thought.

"And how about the mouse?" Karpfen asked. "Is it still alive?"

"Sure," said Tony. "I've got it hidden under my bed."

Karpfen didn't seem surprised, but Dr. Neugeboren was outraged.

"We've got enough mice here as it is," he said, "without people taking them in as pets!"

"Helga's a really good mouse," said Tony. "And clean. No one ever complains about her."

He realized, of course, that now it was his duty to explain to the men why he had Helga, and talk them into joining the society. But he just wasn't feeling up to it. If Ernie were alive, he thought, or Albie Feld were here, I could convince them in no time flat. But on his own, he didn't dare.

"Anyway," said Karpfen, poking at Ernie, "it's funny, us standing here, about to bury the boy. It's that goddamn German logic. Die in peace and quiet and they burn you in the crematorium. But do something wrong and they give you a dignified burial."

"I guess the graveyard is supposed to serve as a warning," said Dr. Neugeboren.

"It sure does," said Karpfen. "Lovers come here at night, and just when they're about to go all the way, they suddenly realize where they are and stop."

"Brr," said Mr. Veselý. "I'd be afraid to come here at night."

"I'm not so sure anyone would come with you, anyway," Karpfen said. "You aren't exactly a spring chicken anymore."

"I would be afraid, too," said Dr. Neugeboren. "And I'm not even superstitious. Cross my heart."

"You they might go for still," said Karpfen. "Even if your armor isn't so shiny anymore. But not to worry. What's the worst that could happen? Some dead guy wakes up, you tell him to lie back down and be quiet," he said to Tony, staring straight ahead at Ernie's legs. "Any of you men want those shoes? They look pretty solid still."

"No," said Dr. Neugeboren. "None of us needs any shoes."

"Don't you think we ought to get started?" Mr. Veselý said with worry. "It's ten o'clock. Who knows who else they might bring in?"

"No, that's it for today," said Karpfen. "I noticed that when there's a transport, not as many people die."

"They say today's the last one," said Mr. Veselý.

"They say that every time," said Dr. Neugeboren.

"But where do they put all those people?" Mr. Veselý wondered. "Our transports aren't the only ones going there."

"The world is deep and wide. Maybe the reason this boy here ran away," Karpfen said, touching Ernie with his pick, "wasn't because of Fifi or the SS-Sturmbahn-führer. Maybe it was because he found out what they're doing with all those Jews."

"What do *you* think they're doing?"

"I don't know," said Karpfen. "But one thing I know for sure. They aren't shooting them."

"That's a relief."

"They aren't shooting them," Karpfen went on, "because the Germans would never waste ammunition like that. Do you have any idea how much it costs to fill a rifle?"

"No," said Mr. Veselý.

"For that much, you could buy three blue Mercurys," said Karpfen.

"They aren't that rare," Mr. Veselý said. "Thirty crowns a stamp, maybe thirty-five."

"So what?" said Karpfen. "You can do the math yourself. Three times thirty is ninety. Almost a hundred crowns per Jew. And according to the latest data, which aren't even complete, in 1938 there were fifteen million

Jews in Europe. So one hundred times fifteen million. That's a lot of money."

"Gentlemen," Dr. Neugeboren reminded them, "he's just a boy."

"Let him learn to count," said Karpfen. "It won't do him any harm."

"I already know how to count," said Tony. He was a little insulted. Arithmetic had always been his strong point in school. It was grammar and art that gave him problems.

"So, tell me, Mr. Karpfen, what do you think they do with them?" said Mr. Veselý.

"I'd say they hang them. But that doesn't seem right, either. Too impractical. Have you ever seen a hanging?"

"Yes," said Mr. Veselý. "Here in the ghetto."[11]

"I was there, too," said Karpfen. "It took at least five minutes for each one, maybe more. Now do the math again. The transports out of the ghetto take a thousand people each, at two-day intervals. But a thousand people—assuming they also worked at night,

11) These executions were conducted with great pomp, in accordance with all the rules valid at the time. However, the Germans were far less concerned with the legalities of the matter than they were with convincing the inhabitants of the ghetto that "not all deaths are equal." Nobody knows to what extent they were successful in this.

which would be pretty unusual—that would take four or five days. And that's not even leaving time for breaks. Forget it. To hang that many people is just plain uneconomical."

"Wouldn't they be worth more to them alive anyway?" said Mr. Veselý, ever the optimist.

"No," said Karpfen. "Most of us can no longer manage the level of output that would make it worthwhile investing in us. Don't forget, the price of food always goes up in wartime."

"You forget," said Dr. Neugeboren, "that luckily there's such a thing as world opinion."

"I'm not forgetting," said Karpfen. "But it seems to me, Doctor, we're rather removed from world opinion. Surely, economics is more of a factor at this point. I've come to the conclusion that they drown the people in water. That's the cheapest way."

"But what about the fish? Wouldn't it bother them?" asked Tony, hoping it might allow him to change the subject back to the SPCA again. Now that he knew the men better, he was sure he could win them over. Mr. Veselý, no problem. Probably Dr. Neugeboren, too. Karpfen he wasn't so sure about. He didn't seem to like animals much.

But Karpfen agreed. "You're a sharp kid, Tony," he said. "Of course, they couldn't do it in a fishpond. The toxins from the corpses might harm the fish. It might totally spoil their breeding. In my opinion, they'd have to use a lake. I bet you could drown a few million Jews in a good-sized lake without too much trouble."

"Most Jews know how to swim," Dr. Neugeboren objected. "Well, I myself don't, but my wife is an excellent swimmer."

"I already thought of that," said Karpfen. "You just throw a net over them. Of course, it would have to be strong, so it wouldn't tear."

"What if someone had a knife?" said Tony, remembering how Ledecký had carved the meat from Fifi's thigh. At least he'd had a good meal, which could only be a help. After all, Ledecký wasn't that strong, and he'd have to do something there. Maybe he could shovel snow, Tony thought. That's pretty hard work. But then again, not *that* hard. The main thing is to keep your shovel moving.

"No problem," said Karpfen. "A couple machine guns would do the trick. They'd have to find a way to get the people in the water. But it wouldn't take nearly as much ammunition as it would if they just up and shot them. In any case, this whole debate is academic. Either we'll be summoned for a transport, in which case we'll see for ourselves, or we won't, in which case, what do we care?"

"None of your relatives have gone yet, have they?" asked Mr. Veselý.

"Sure, they have," said Karpfen. "But will it help them for me sit here conjecturing on what might or might not have happened? No, it won't."

"I guess you're right," said Mr. Veselý. "But now, gentlemen, I really do think we ought to get moving so that . . ."

"Yeah, yeah, we're moving, we're moving," said Karpfen, slowly getting to his feet. "The ground isn't frozen yet. We'll be done in a jiffy."

"That's right," said Dr. Neugeboren. He stood up as well. "In two hours, we'll be home free. But if you don't mind, Mr. Karpfen, could you watch where you swing that pick? It isn't a toy, you know."

Mr. Veselý relaxed. He trusted men with academic titles. Thanks to his former profession, he knew where British Guyana, Honduras, and Tasmania were. But men like them, they knew the world.

CHAPTER 9

IN WHICH HELGA GETS A NEW BOX

By the time Tony returned to L 315, Nurse Anna was on duty.

But, apart from her, the only ones in the room were Mr. Glaser and Sons and Mr. Adamson.

Nurse Anna was sitting on Mr. Brisch's empty bed.

That's strange, Tony thought. Nurse Anna, unlike Nurse Maria Louisa, would allow visitors to sit on the bed, but never did so herself. It was a rule she adhered to rigorously.

"So, what do you say, Tony?" said Mr. Glaser and Sons. "I had a feeling. My words came to pass. I was right. It's terrible."

Tony didn't say anything. He had no idea what Mr. Glaser and Sons was talking about. Then suddenly he recalled that Nurse Maria Louisa had complained about Mr. Brisch calling her a whore. Of course, she had called him a pig first, but Tony wasn't sure whether calling a former nun a whore was worse than calling a former violinist a pig. Or maybe what had offended her was the fact that Mr. Brisch had addressed her using the informal "you."

Besides, Tony knew from experience that girls were far more sensitive than guys when it came to being called names. Probably because they knew that guys would always stick up for them. If Nurse Maria Louisa had complained to the head doctor, he wouldn't even have bothered to hear the other side's point of view; he would have just summoned Mr. Brisch on the spot and given him a dressing-down. Tony knew how these things worked.

"Truly terrible," said Nurse Anna, bursting into tears.

It was a strange sight to see. Nurse Anna crying while Mr. Adamson prayed. Tony had a sudden urge to hide Mr. Adamson's prayer straps. Just to see if he would still rock back and forth and mumble like that without them. I should have done it a long time ago, he thought. I should have hidden them someplace hard to find. Maybe he would get over the habit. Or maybe at least he wouldn't make such a big deal out of it.

Then suddenly Tony got worried: What if something bad had happened to Helga? He had been busy burying Ernie all day and completely forgot about her. What if she'd chewed through the box and run away? Or what if Mr. Brisch had lost his temper and tossed her on the trash heap along with the box? He'd threatened to do it more than once. But no, he wouldn't do that, Tony thought. Even if he did call her names, he was actually fond of her. And besides, if something bad had happened to Helga, it would make sense for Nurse Anna to cry, but Mr. Glaser and Sons wouldn't be saying it was terrible. On the other hand, he didn't think it was likely that Nurse Anna would cry just because Mr. Brisch had gotten a dressing-down from the doctor.

So, instead of trying to figure it out on his own, Tony asked, "Where are the other men?"

"You mean you don't know?" said Mr. Glaser and Sons. "Where do you think?"

"In the latrine?" Tony said. Then he realized that made no sense. Why would they all go to the latrine together? Plus, lately Professor Steinbach had been relieving himself in a bowl. His health wasn't so good. They must be getting an X-ray then, Tony concluded.

"This is no time for jokes," said Mr. Glaser and Sons. "They left on the transport. All of them. We were afraid that you did too, given that you were gone for so long."

"No," said Tony. "I didn't." He started to worry about Helga again. If Mr. Brisch, Mr. Löwy, and Professor Steinbach, her main supporters, had left, who knew what had happened to her? Mr. Glaser and Sons couldn't be trusted. And Nurse Anna was just one big ball of tears.

He peeked inside the box.

Helga was still there. She just seemed a little tired. Of course she is, thought Tony, seeing as nobody bothered to take her out for a walk all day. He gingerly lifted her out of the box and asked Nurse Anna if it would be all right for him to put Helga down for a while on one of the beds that used to belong to the men. "In the box, of course," he added, noticing Nurse Anna's frown. "I just think it would do her good. She'd get more light that way than under the bed."

Mr. Glaser and Sons was outraged. "How can you talk about a mouse at a time like this? You heard what Nurse Anna said. The men left on the transport: the professor, Mr. Löwy, and that German."

"Mr. Brisch," said Tony, correcting him.

"That German," Mr. Glaser and Sons repeated stubbornly. People say you should only speak well of the dead and of those who aren't present. But Mr. Glaser and Sons didn't abide by that maxim. Maybe because Mr. Brisch hadn't been gone that long.

"The worst part is," Nurse Anna said, wiping her nose, "the doctor left too. Who's going to give the patients their pneumothorax treatment now?"

"As far as I know, almost no one still here has it," said Mr. Glaser and Sons. "I know I don't. And Tony here doesn't either."

"I used to," Tony said.

"But what if somebody gets sick and needs treatment?" said Nurse Anna. "Dr. Kleinhamplová doesn't know how. She's never done it before. This is terrible."

"We can only hope that doesn't happen," said Mr. Glaser and Sons. "Or they'll just have to get better the old-fashioned way: Eat well and get plenty of rest."

"But you know the food in the ghetto doesn't provide enough calories. And the patients won't stay in bed. They're so undisciplined."

"I can stick to it," said Tony. "And so can Helga." He was trying to make Nurse Anna happy. But it didn't seem to work.

"It's the worst misfortune that could befall us," she said. "He was doing important scientific work. And he didn't even take his underclothes with him. He left his robe here, too."

"He won't be needing a robe where he's going," said Mr. Glaser and Sons. "I'm sure they don't wear robes there."

"But still," Nurse Anna said. "At least if he'd brought some clean shirts, so he could change. He's going to get lice."

"In my experience," said Mr. Glaser and Sons, "if a person is clean, he doesn't get lice. Even if he's got only one shirt."

"He probably has more than one. His other suitcase had two, I think, and he was wearing one."

"I'm sure he's got more than one. Imagine a head

doctor with only one shirt," said Mr. Glaser and Sons. "I'd like to see that."

"But still," said Nurse Anna. "It's so sad here now. With the gentlemen gone. The room is so empty."

"I can let Helga out," Tony said. "Once she starts running around, the room will seem full right away. You'll see."

But Nurse Anna said no. Tony got the feeling she was still afraid of Helga. But he was convinced it was only because she didn't know her well enough. If she knew her better, she wouldn't be afraid of her, Tony was sure. After all, it wasn't as if she would hurt anyone.

What Tony didn't know, as we already revealed, was that every woman is scared of mice. And Nurse Anna was no exception. Besides which, she was just too sad.

"For me this room is going to seem empty forever," she said.

"Me too," said Mr. Glaser and Sons. "The question is whether that means I should mourn. If you look at it objectively, it's actually a good thing if not all the beds in the hospital are occupied. Not only does it attest to a general level of health, but it also leaves more room for us."

"That's a pretty sad joke, Mr. Glaser," said Nurse Anna.

"What joke?" said Mr. Glaser and Sons. "Think about it. In some rooms there were as many as twenty-five Jews at a time. That certainly isn't healthy. Not to mention, you had TB patients together with asthmatics, diabetics with jaundice patients, young boys with old men. That couldn't be good for anyone. At least this way, you'll be able to sort them out a little."

"There weren't that many young people left," said Tony. "All the cooks left on the last transport."

"That isn't that much of a loss," said Mr. Glaser and Sons. "At least there won't be so much stealing."

"So who's going to cook?" said Tony.

"Someone will turn up," said Mr. Glaser and Sons. "Everyone knows what a good job it is. You can eat your fill and still walk away with as much as you can carry."

Tony didn't bother to argue. It was no use. Mr. Glaser and Sons was biased against cooks. Most of the ghetto's inhabitants were biased against them. How many times had Tony tried to explain to people that Ernie and Ledecký were ordinary human beings, just like them, only instead of working in a factory or office, they worked in a kitchen. His arguments were in vain. Everyone saw them sort of like they used to see aristocrats.

Though when you think about it, Tony said to himself, the aristocrats weren't that different, either. Look at Ledecký. You could barely tell him apart from the other cooks. Except that he was a little shorter. But that wasn't because he was an aristocrat. Mr. Brisch claimed that all aristocrats were degenerate. But you couldn't always take Mr. Brisch literally.

Tony took the big box out from under Mr. Löwy's bed and looked through it. Mr. Löwy had used it to hide bread in. Not that he had that much, but he always said, with a big box, at least that way he could imagine he did. Tony thought it might be nice for Helga. Her box was starting to fall apart, and besides, this one was much more spacious, so she would have more room to move around. Just need to make a few holes, to let the air in, Tony thought.

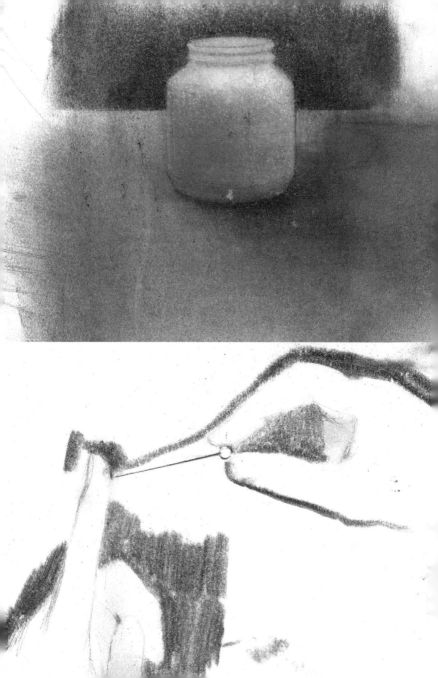

CHAPTER 10

IN WHICH TONY PRICKS HIS FINGER

Nurse Anna's fears that Dr. Kleinhamplová wouldn't be able to cope with the influx of new patients turned out to be unfounded.

There were no new patients.

With the transports going on, no one was in the mood to come in for an X-ray just because they had a cough and night sweats.

Tony remained alone in the room with Mr. Adamson and Mr. Glaser and Sons.

It seemed unnaturally quiet. Every now and then Mr. Adamson prayed, and occasionally Mr. Glaser and Sons chided Tony, but it just wasn't the same.

As a result, Tony was glad even when his mother came to visit.

She hadn't shown her face in L 315 much recently.

His mother was actually famous for how well she could pack. So she was always on the move. People would ask her to come look at their suitcase or rucksack and tell them how they could arrange things better.

Today, too, she looked like she was in a hurry.

At least it seemed that way to Tony.

When he looked at her more closely, though, he could tell she was upset.

"What's wrong?" he asked. "Don't tell me Eddie Spitz is on the transport."

"Eddie Spitz? No, he left already three days ago." She stared off into the space behind Tony's back.

"Are you sad?" Tony asked.

"Yes," said his mother. "But that doesn't matter now. There's something I need to tell you. You're a big boy now, right?"

"Me? Not really. I'm still only five foot four. I haven't even grown an inch the past year. It's probably the food."

"Tony, stop kidding around. You know that's not what I mean."

But Tony wasn't kidding. It genuinely bothered him. Five feet four inches wasn't very tall. It was all right for now, but once he hit seventeen, then what? He would be a small fry.

His mother wasn't referring to his height, though. "What I was getting at is, you're old enough now that I can tell you anything, right?"

"Sure," Tony said.

"Then please don't be alarmed, but I came to tell you, we're both on it."

"Now that's a surprise," said Tony. It suddenly hit him that the summons for the transport didn't apply only to him and his mother, but Helga too. He began to get worried. If it had been a week ago, it wouldn't have been that bad. The men may have called Helga names, but when they found out Tony was leaving, he was sure one of them would have taken care of her. But the men weren't here anymore. Mr. Glaser and Sons didn't count. And forget about Mr. Adamson.

"I haven't received the summons yet," Tony's mother said, "but I got it from reliable sources. It'll come this afternoon."

"So there's nothing we can do," said Tony.

He knew people did all sorts of things. In the morning, five hundred people had their names on the transport; by afternoon, there would be fifty left and the remaining four hundred and fifty had been replaced by four hundred and fifty others. But that was just at first, when there were more people in the ghetto and having a profession protected you. If you were a doctor, say, or a cook or a musician or a butcher. Of course that also meant people pretended to be doctors or cooks (or musicians or butchers), or even their relatives, to help them get out of it. But on the last few transports, none of those privileges had done anyone any good.

"That's why I came to see you," said Liza. She said they weren't accepting any exemptions at all for the transport. Not even if you worked at Magdeburg Barracks. There was a time when that had been the most reliable way to get out. "Not to mention the cooks and butchers and bakers," she added sadly. They had been slotted for the earlier transports. Tony already knew that. "This time it won't even help if you're wracked with cancer," his mother said. "You could even be related to the King of England. The only thing that'll work is if you can prove you're so sick that you wouldn't even make it alive to the Sudetenlands, where everyone boards the train."

"You'd have to be pretty far gone for that," said Tony. "You'd have to have a heart attack, or be spitting blood."

"That's right," said Liza. "You have to fake it, Tony. That's the only way they'll exempt you."

"You too," Tony said.[12]

"Maybe, honey. But this isn't about me."

12) On family transports, if one family member was summoned, the whole family went, and, by the same token, if one family member was exempted, the whole family was exempted along with them. This system had both advantages and disadvantages. One advantage was that the whole family went together—although this wasn't always an advantage, and it wasn't an advantage for everyone. One disadvantage was that it interfered with the uniformity of the transports—if, for example, a transport was composed of lawyers and traveling salesmen, or craftsmen and tuberculosis patients—since it meant that family members went who weren't of that profession, or didn't have that illness.

"My heart is totally healthy," said Tony. He was surprised to hear his mother use that term of endearment. She hadn't called him that since he was just a little boy. "But I might be able to do it. I saw Mr. Kauders from room 2 die of a heart attack. I don't think any doctor would fall for it, though. Not even Dr. Kleinhamplová."

"I don't want you to fake a heart attack," said Liza. "What you need to do is spit blood." She handed him a safety pin and showed him the spot on his index finger where he should prick himself. "You just have to suck out a little bit, then spit it into a handkerchief or a spittoon."

"I don't think blood from your lungs looks the same as blood from your finger. The doctor might be able to tell," said Tony.

But his mother said she had already spoken to Dr. Kleinhamplová, and she was in on it. The SS-Sturmbannführer would be the one checking, so the blood was for him. "They say this is the last transport," said Liza.

Tony didn't understand the logic, but he got that the SS-Sturmbannführer wouldn't be able to tell the difference.

"I'll ask Mr. Glaser and Sons to hold my hand while I prick myself," he said.

His mother disagreed. "I'm sorry, Tony, honey, but Mr. Glaser isn't allowed to know."

"Then I'll ask Mr. Adamson." Tony couldn't imagine how he would explain it to him, and he wasn't sure if Mr. Adamson would even do it. What if pricking yourself in the finger with a safety pin was against the Jewish religion? But he figured he might as well ask. It didn't cost anything.

His mother didn't agree to that, either. "No one's allowed to know," she said. "It's bad enough that I had to tell Dr. Kleinhamplová. You'll just have to do it yourself."

"All right then," said Tony. But he wasn't sure if he could. One time he had tried to cut himself with a knife, so he knew how hard it was. His mother gave him an unusually dramatic hug and made him promise one more time not to forget anything. She had an urge to repeat it all over again, but she knew Tony knew what it looked like when a person was spewing blood.

She gave him an encouraging wink as she remembered the time they had put Tony in the dying room. He was extremely uneasy, until he and his mother began making bets on which patient would die first. One, a Danish man, had been vomiting blood.

In the end, they took Tony out of the room. He too was spitting up blood from time to time, but it turned out it wasn't that bad. He and his mother often remembered the Danish man after that. Tony had guessed correctly not only his day, but even the hour.

Tony's mother left and Tony gave himself a prick beneath the pillow, wondering if he should test it out first. He had plenty of time till that afternoon, when the SS-Sturmbannführer would come, to learn how to spit and prick himself in the finger to make sure he bled. But then he thought it might actually be better not to test it, since the SS-Sturmbannführer might look at his hand and see the prick marks on his fingers. Generally, the Germans didn't come that close to Jews, but what with it being the last transport, you never knew. Besides, as long as he pricked himself once or twice, he ought to have plenty of blood.

That afternoon, a general confusion ensued.

Nurse Anna kept coming by to make sure the sheets weren't poking out of the beds.

Nurse Maria Louisa came to see if the thermometers were on the nightstands, where they were supposed to be.

Even the head nurse came to visit, fluffing the pillow on Mr. Brisch's former bed with her very own hands.

Tony wasn't happy. Not that he had anything against tidiness in principle, but slowly but surely the time was approaching when he would have to prick himself, and with someone coming into the room all the time, it got in his way.

His mother had emphasized that she didn't want any witnesses.

Apart from that, Mr. Glaser and Sons acted as if the SS-Sturmbannführer was coming just for him and that Tony was in the way of his preparations for this rare visit.

"Don't even think about blowing your nose while he's here," said Mr. Glaser and Sons. "He might consider it an act of provocation. And you mustn't cough either. The SS always see people who cough as suspicious. Sometimes our people use coughs to communicate with each other. And they know that. They know us."

"I'm just going to lie here nice and quiet," Tony said.

He was being serious. If you want to fake spitting blood, you have to lie down nice and quiet, staying on your back, and not move around at all.

Finally, things quieted down for a while, so Tony sat up on the headboard and tried to prick himself in the finger.

Keeping his back turned to Mr. Glaser, of course.

Mr. Glaser and Sons assumed that Tony was trimming his nails, and began lamenting the fact that he was dirtying the floor with his clippings.

Tony found it annoying, but even worse, as he had

feared, he couldn't manage to prick himself properly. No matter how he tried, his hand would always jerk away. He moved the pin from left hand to right and right hand to left, but it was no use. His hand jerked out of the way every time. He tried resting his left hand on his knee and boring a hole through the pillow with the safety pin to his middle finger, which was the one that seemed best, but it still didn't work. The safety pin was too dull and his skin was like rubber. Instead of a hole he could suck blood from, it just made a sort of blue indentation in his finger.

Then Mr. Glaser and Sons started going on again, so Tony tried to do it in bed, underneath the blanket. But as soon as Mr. Glaser and Sons noticed, he said Tony was too big a boy to be playing under the covers like that, who knew what he was getting up to, and his bed looked like a Gypsy camp.

Tony, who wasn't able to do it under the covers either (his hand still kept jumping out of the way), got up and went to the toilet.

He didn't have any success there either. He wasn't afraid of the pain—he'd been given more injections already than he could count—it just didn't work. His hand wouldn't obey him.

Some might argue there was no need to put himself to so much trouble. He could have scraped his gums and it would have worked as well or better, since instead of having to suck out the blood, he could just spit it straight in the spittoon. Tony realized that afterward. But it's often the case that we don't think of the best solution until we no longer need it. There was also the fact that his mother had brought him the safety pin and told him to prick his finger. Tony wanted to accommodate her and didn't give too much thought to whether there might be some other way to go about it. The whole thing made him sad.

My mother is going to go on the transport and Helga's going to die, all because of my twitchy hand, Tony thought.

Then Mr. Glaser and Sons said: "Here he comes."

Tony didn't hear a thing, but the whole building fell quiet. It looked like Mr. Glaser and Sons had been right. They must have gotten word next door that the SS-Sturmbannführer was on his way, because otherwise the men in numbers 24 and 25 would have been talking still. The men in room 24 especially; they were terrible chatterboxes.

I've got to do something quick, but what? Tony thought. He was soaked with sweat trying to figure out what to do. Then it came to him.

It was a silly trick, but it just might work.

Yesterday he had been issued a portion of jam. There was still a spoonful left.

It was red, after all. It might look like blood in the spittoon. He felt kind of bad about sacrificing the jam. They didn't get it often, at most once every three months, but he really wanted to do as his mother had asked. She's already done so much for me, he thought. She's fed me this whole time. At one point, he calculated that she had brought him more than fifty dumplings during their time in the ghetto. So this one time she asked him for something, he couldn't let her down. For Helga's sake too.

He attempted one last time to prick himself in the finger, but again his hand jerked out of the way, so he took the spoon and dropped the jam into the spittoon.

As long as the SS-Sturmbannführer doesn't try to smell it, he won't be able to tell, Tony thought.

Suddenly he began to think he'd made a mistake. Instead of dropping the jam straight in the spittoon, he should have at least rolled it around in his mouth a while. But then again, he thought, who knows, maybe the jam's artificially colored and it would have lost its color. I was right to do what I did. After that, he just kept his fingers crossed that the SS-Sturmbannführer wouldn't be able to tell.

The SS-Sturmbannführer didn't notice a thing.

How could he, when all he did was pass by the door? Afterward, Mr. Glaser and Sons claimed that he heard

Dr. Kleinhamplová deliver a report. Allegedly she said, in German: "That's Mr. Glaser, cavity on the left side the size of a plum," but Tony and the men from room 24 didn't believe his story. They said if Dr. Kleinhamplová had actually delivered a report, she wouldn't have said "Mr. Glaser," but at best simply "Glaser," and more likely "Glaser the Jew," in accordance with regulations. They also had serious doubts whether the SS-Sturmbannführer cared one way or the other that Mr. Glaser had a cavity the size of a plum. Not to mention, they all knew he didn't have a cavity the size of a plum on the left side of his mouth. It was just decay, with extensive suppuration on the right, and he was trying to keep it a secret from them. And that was how Tony, his mother, Liza, and his mouse, Helga, got out of the last transport.

CHAPTER 11
IN WHICH WE LEARN MAINLY
ABOUT THE BRUTALITY OF HORST MUNTHER
AND THE LONELINESS OF NURSE LILI

The sun was shining over the ghetto. When the sun shines over the ghetto, that's good.

The puddles glittered in the streets, and the metal tower of the Catholic church seemed even more metallic than usual.

Tony had moved into the Engineers' Barracks and now had a view of the tower right from his bed. It didn't give him a religious feeling to look at it, though. Usually it just reminded him of their unsuccessful field trip in search of pigeons, and then he would think about how the Tausiks had eaten them. He still felt bad about that.

Sometimes he would sit on the windowsill and watch the traffic on the street. Whenever there was any. After the transports in the fall, the ghetto had lost four fifths of its population and it was deserted and sad.

Apart from that, Tony was worried about Helga.

When they put him in the Engineers' Barracks, they had assigned a room with Horst Munther. It was just the two of them, and Tony was afraid that one of these times, when he went away, Horst would do something bad to Helga. Once he got his hooks into her, that would be the end of that.

Fortunately, though, for some reason Horst had so far left her alone.

On the other hand, he didn't leave Tony alone for even a second.

At first, he just lay in bed all day, staring up at the ceiling. Soon, however, he came up with an entertaining pastime, inventing German terms of abuse and showering Tony with them. Tony had to admit his roommate was incredibly inventive and persistent. So much so, he thought he must have set the world record for swearing, right here in the ghetto.

Sometimes he would beat Tony, too.

The first part didn't bother Tony that much, since he didn't understand German too well, but the second part was pretty unpleasant. Horst was a strong guy, plus he was learning to box.

He swore constantly, under his breath, even when Nurse Lili from L 315 came to see Tony.

The hospital personnel hadn't moved into the Engineers' Barracks. Only the patients.

But Tony refused to let his roommate spoil the visit. Nurse Lili may know some German, he said to himself, but she certainly didn't know the expressions Horst was using.

As it happened, Tony underestimated the nurse's linguistic knowledge.

"How are you?" she said as she sat down next to Tony on the bed. As a nurse, she was allowed to do that. She could also come and go outside of visiting hours.

"Fine," Tony said.

She glanced around the room. "Pretty swanky here," she said. "Double room."

"We've even got running water," Tony said proudly, pointing to a small metal container over the washbasin with a faucet attached to it. They brought the water inside from a well, but still, it was like running water.

"That's swell," said Nurse Lili. "I can come over to your place to wash up."

"Just as long as he doesn't mind." Tony gestured to Horst with his eyes.

"He won't," she said without looking his way. By this point, she had developed a skill for talking about people who didn't understand her in their presence. "You don't know men like I do. They're glad to have women come wash up at their place. That way they can tell everyone they peeked through the keyhole at them. Even if there isn't any keyhole to peek through."

"But he might be different," Tony said. He might not care if there's a keyhole or not, Tony thought. He might just break down the door.

"They're all the same," said Nurse Lili with an air of experience. "Don't worry. Are you going to introduce us?"

The idea didn't appeal to Tony at all. "I can't," he said. "He doesn't speak Czech."

That much was true. When Horst went to school, he hadn't learned the language of that little country in central Europe. For that matter, he hadn't even gone to school that much.

"Plus he's pretty steamed up," Tony said. "He's in here by mistake."

"You mean he doesn't have TB? Well, we can easily check. Just bring him in for an X-ray. Dr. Kleinhamplová's no expert, but she can tell if somebody's got tuberculosis or not."

Tony was surprised. He wasn't used to hearing such confident statements from Lili. That was more Albie Feld's style, or Ernie's. It's probably because there aren't that many men here anymore, he decided.

"No, that's not what I meant. He has TB. It's a mistake that he's here in the ghetto. He was a member of the Hitlerjugend, until they found out he had a Jewish grandpa.[13] Only he claims it wasn't his grandpa."

"So whose grandpa was he?" Nurse Lili asked. She didn't like the idea of someone disavowing their grand-

13) The Germans followed the Nuremberg Laws to the letter. Once they found out you had Jewish blood, it didn't matter whether you were a maharaja or an SS-Obergruppenführer. Either way, you went on the transport.

father. She had always acknowledged hers, even if he was just an ordinary kosher butcher.

"Nobody knows. Probably no one's. Though I guess that's impossible. He must have been somebody's grandpa. He must have had at least one grandson, if he was a grandfather."

"Of course," said Nurse Lili. She sized up the Jewish member of the Hitler Youth with a scornful look. A boy who disavowed his own grandfather. She wasn't impressed, even if he did weigh two hundred pounds. "His grandma was fine," said Tony. "But she must have been the kind of woman who argues a lot. Assuming he gets it from her, that is." He unconsciously touched his hand to the bruise on his forehead.

"How do you two argue, then, if you don't understand each other?"

"Sometimes we communicate with our hands."

It looked more like Horst Munther communicated some things to Tony with his fists.

"Does he beat you up?" Lili asked. She didn't have too much experience with that. Usually, she was on duty in the urology and tuberculosis units, not surgery, and besides, there weren't too many fistfights in the ghetto. When there was one, it was usually civilized enough that no one ended up in the hospital.

"Yes," Tony admitted. "I think it's because I don't

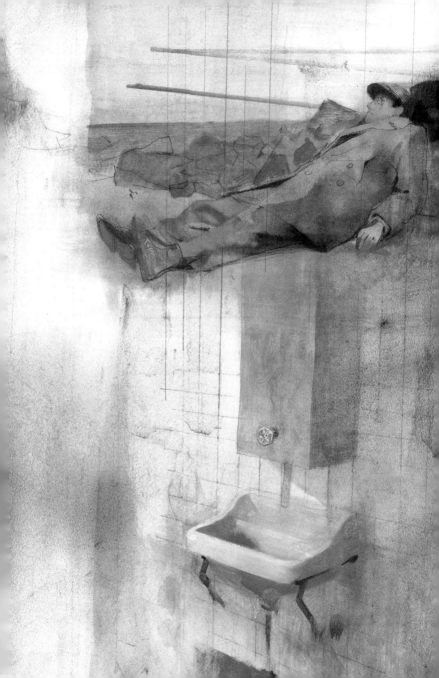

really understand him. If I did, I'm sure he wouldn't beat me up. Except for that, though, I get along with him pretty well."

"That's not what it looks like from your forehead. Looks more like you ran into the ramparts."

"It's no big deal," Tony said. "As soon as my German's good enough, he'll stop beating me up."

"I hope so," said Lili.

"For sure," Tony said. "See, because then I'll get him to join our society. And as a member of our society, he can't beat up another member."

Tony had been trying on a near daily basis to convince Horst to join the SPCA. But he knew only a few German expressions, plus Ochs (ox), Esel (donkey), and Schwein (pig), and the fragmentary sentences that he could put together using those words were hardly enough for Horst to understand the matter in its full breadth. In fact, just the opposite, often, when Tony would start a conversation, using the few words at his disposal, Horst, being the suspicious type, assumed he was insulting him. The last time it had happened was just the day before, when Tony remembered the German counting rhyme: Und die Kuh, das bist du. Horst took the mention of "cow" personally, and immediately reacted by trying to take the violin that Tony had from Mr. Brisch and throw it out the window. When Tony tried to pull it back, Horst snarled, "du Saujud," and pounced on him.

That was how he got the bruise.

The more Tony familiarized her with the nuances of Horst's personality, the less freely Nurse Lili felt to speak around him. "I'd like a word alone with you," she said one day to Tony.

"But I'm telling you, honestly, he doesn't understand."

Not only was Tony convinced that his roommate wouldn't understand what they said anyway, but he couldn't figure out how to ask him to leave. Even if he did do a decent job of explaining, which wasn't likely considering his language skills, it still didn't mean Horst would do as he asked. Probably just the opposite.

But as it turned out, Tony misjudged him. Horst realized, without being told, that his presence wasn't welcome, and after a while he stood up and began to get dressed.

"Ich geh in die Stadt," he grumbled as he moved toward the door.

"Auf Wiedersehen," Nurse Lili said.

"Scheisse," Horst said, slamming the door behind him.

Clearly, he wasn't used to talking to girls.

He did have a sister, though. She came to visit every week, and even though she usually did most of the talking, he also sometimes talked to her.

"Sie ist eine jüdische Hure," he said of her as she walked out the door after her last visit.

How could he call his own sister a Jewish whore when he claimed to be a pure-blooded Aryan? Tony couldn't get it out of his head for days afterward. Unless maybe she was his stepsister, Tony concluded.

Apart from that, Tony quite liked Horst's sister. She didn't talk much, but what she said carried weight. Tony could tell, even if he didn't understand. And she had a special way of walking. A swing in her hips or something.

Once Horst left, Nurse Lili breathed an audible sigh of relief.

"That is one dangerous individual," she said in her new, important-sounding voice.

"Don't be mad at him," Tony said. "He's a good guy at heart. Just a little foulmouthed. When he joins our society, I'm going to put him in charge of wild animals. Originally, I was going to give him the domestic cat, but he might take a swing at it, and then the whole thing would be ruined. But he won't be able to do any harm to a wild animal."

"Let's hope not," Nurse Lili said.

"I guarantee it. He wouldn't dare take on a lion

or tiger. But I'm boring you with all this animal talk, aren't I?"

"Not at all," said Lili, sliding closer. "I'm interested in everything you do."

Tony inched away. He didn't like it when people sat too close to him on the bed. Especially not when they were sitting on top of his covers.

"I don't really do that much. Just lie around and peek in at Helga every once in a while."

It wasn't entirely true. There were the occasional run-ins with Horst, as previously mentioned. But he didn't see any reason to talk about that. He'd already said enough on that subject.

He asked Lili if she'd like to have a look at Helga.

She didn't seem too interested. "I already saw her," she said.

It wasn't just an excuse—she'd actually come to see Helga right when he first got her—but it was in part, given that it had been at least three months since then, and in three months a mouse can change considerably. Tony was quick to point that out. "You wouldn't believe how much she's grown. She's a totally different mouse now! Seriously, let me show you," said Tony, leaning down from the bed to pull out the box.

Nurse Lili reached out and grabbed his arm. "Wait," she said. "What if she's sleeping?"

"Then we'll wake her up. She'll be glad, you'll see. She likes having visitors."

"I'd really rather you didn't wake her. I'm not in the mood today." Nurse Lili took out a mirror and comb and began fixing her hair.

Clearly she had other concerns.

"All right then," said Tony. "But I'll show you next time. For sure."

"I'll be ready," said Nurse Lili. "And I'll bring her some grains."

But she still didn't seem to be looking forward to it that much. So Tony changed the subject and asked how things were in L 315. "What's new over there?" he said.

"What would there be? Same as ever."

"Is Nurse Maria Louisa still mad at Mr. Brisch?"

"No," said Nurse Lili. "Whatever gave you that idea? She never stays mad that long at anyone. She always forgives them, like a good Christian. That's the worst thing about her, stupid cow."

"What about the men?" asked Tony. He didn't like hearing one nurse talk about another that way. "Is Mr. Adamson still praying?"

"No, not anymore. He went on the last transport too, if you can imagine. And on Saturday of all days, Shabbes. At first he said he wasn't going anywhere. He said, 'On Saturdays I don't even go for a walk.' Then he changed his mind and went. But he griped and complained the whole way."

"That's sad," Tony said.

But Mr. Adamson's behavior wasn't actually sad, so much as natural. In certain situations, as Mr. Löwy used to say, people think more of people than of God. If someone slaps you in the face, you don't think of it as a slap from God. You say it was Mr. Lederer, or Mr. Jajteles, or Mr. Štědrý. If for no other reason than you can't slap God back, but you can hit Mr. Lederer, Mr. Jajteles, or Mr. Štědrý. It's the same when you end up on a transport. You know it wasn't the Lord who put you there, but the SS men in ghetto headquarters. And there's no saving yourself from them. So Shabbes or not, you go, and you just try not to draw too much attention from God.

"So what is Mr. Glaser and Sons up to?" asked Tony. "Is he still offended all the time?"

"All the time," said Nurse Lili.

"That's just how some people are. Like Horst here," Tony said, tossing his head in his roommate's direction.

"You're right. The boys were never like that. Especially not Ernie. Even if there were lots of times when I wished he would get offended. At least for my sake, if not his. But he never did."

"You can't blame him," Tony said. "I guess it takes talent. And Ernie just didn't have it. Horst, on the other hand, seems to have a special gift when it comes to taking offense. I've also noticed the stronger person is always the only one."

"Why shouldn't weaker people get upset too?" Nurse Lili asked.

"They can. It just doesn't do them any good. So it's better not to. Especially if they're on their own."

"You miss the boys, huh?"

"Really bad," said Tony. "Horst Munther just isn't the same."

"I met a Dutch boy, over in the butcher's shop, where Jenda Schleim used to work. But he wasn't the same either."

"Jenda was a good one, huh?"

"Sure was."

"Maybe he would have turned out to be a great actor. Remember how well he played that lazy guy? And in real life he wasn't lazy one bit! That was more Albie Feld's thing."

"I'd vouch for Albie any day."

"Me too," said Tony. "I'm just saying he was a tad, you know, overconfident. At times. Don't you think?"

"We all have our flaws. But it never went anywhere with that Dutch boy. We couldn't even communicate.

And they gossiped about us anyway. People are always looking for dirt."

"That's true. But if you want to come and wash up at our place, I can heat you up some water. Horst is gone now, so it's no problem."

"You're so naïve," Nurse Lili said, stroking Tony's hair. Apparently she didn't need to wash at the moment.

"I guess I am. I wouldn't be so serious about our SPCA otherwise."

"It's because you have a kind heart," said Lili. She took his hand in hers.

Tony liked the way that felt. It reminded him of when he used to shake hands sometimes with Ernie.

"Not really," he said. "Some people are a lot nicer."

"You're a nice boy. I can tell from the way you take care of that mouse."

"Helga, I have to take care of her. She'd die otherwise. You sure you don't want to see her? You really wouldn't believe how much weight she's put on."

"No, I'm sure. I would just feel sorry for her. I'd be jealous."

"Oh, go on," Tony said. "Why would you be jealous of Helga? You of all people, Lili."

"Well, for instance, the fact that she put on weight. And here I am withering away."

"Actually," said Tony, "you look pretty good."

"No, I don't." She squeezed Tony's hand and shifted away from him on the bed. "I'm getting uglier every day. Don't think I don't know."

Women are so silly, Tony thought. She could just look at herself in the mirror and see that she still looks the same. But out loud he said, "Are you kidding? You, ugly? You're the prettiest girl I know."

Nurse Lili was clearly flattered. "Well, what do you know? Tony paid me a compliment. You say you're just a boy, but you sound grown-up to me."

Tony didn't feel grown-up. And he told her right away why. He thought grown-ups had to have fixed opinions on things. But he had only one opinion, and that was that he was in favor of the society for the prevention of cruelty to animals. And when you thought about it, the society for the prevention of cruelty to animals didn't have a clear opinion either. For example, he had wracked his brains a long time trying to decide whether or not a hunter could be a member of the SPCA. At first he thought no, since they shoot rabbits and all. But then he realized, in winter, hunters feed animals. He couldn't make up his mind.

And not only that. He couldn't arrange anything. For instance, when his mother's boyfriend, Eddie Spitz, went away. He knew it upset her. But he couldn't find her anyone to replace him. "If I were a grown-up," Tony said, "I'm sure I could have arranged it."

"You think?" said Nurse Lili.

"Why not?" Tony said. "There must be a way."

"Hm," said Nurse Lili. "I suppose you're right. Everyone has to arrange things for themselves, one way or another. I get so sad for you sometimes, Tony."

She moved closer to him again, squeezing his hand in one hand and stroking his hair with the other.

Just then, a rustling sound came from under the bed.

"What's that?" said Nurse Lili.

"Oh, nothing. Just Helga," said Tony. "She probably woke up. She isn't used to people sitting on the bed."

"I see," said Nurse Lili. She squeezed his hand harder.

Tony found it pleasant. She wasn't particularly strong, anyway.

Helga kept rustling, louder and louder.

"Couldn't you just put her outside the door for a while?" Nurse Lili asked.

"I'm sorry but no," said Tony. "We keep the temperature steady in here, and she's gotten used to it now. If I put her out in the hallway, she might catch cold."

"I see," said Nurse Lili. "But she won't crawl out of the box, will she? I would get really scared if she did." She stopped stroking Tony's hair and took his other hand in hers.

"No, she won't. And even if she did, there's nothing to be afraid of. I would put her back right away. I've got a lot of practice."

"That's good," said Nurse Lili.

She was clearly impressed by Tony's calm decisiveness.

"You see," she said. "You are a grown-up."

"No, I just seem that way," said Tony. But he was pleased to hear it.

They sat in silence a moment, then Tony spoke up again. "You know, even though I've got Helga now, I still think about Fifi sometimes. I think it was wrong for the boys to eat her. Don't you?"

"Yeah," said Nurse Lili. But her mind was obviously elsewhere.

"Maybe it's because I'm not grown-up yet," said Tony, "but I don't think it's right for people to eat dogs, especially not dogs like Fifi."

"No."

"Am I squeezing your hand too hard?" Tony asked.

"No."

"I wouldn't want to hurt you. I think, in general, people shouldn't hurt each other. Or animals either."

He wasn't being entirely honest. In reality, he was happy to hold one of Lili's hands. But it seemed kind of silly to him to hold both of her hands for so long.

Nurse Lili seemed content, though. In fact she moved even closer to him.

"Just a second," he said. "I need to take my temperature."

Of course he needed at least his right hand to take his temperature.

So Nurse Lili let go of it.

"Have you been running a temperature?" she asked with concern.

"No, but they keep a pretty close eye on it here. We sometimes take our temperature as much as three times a day."

"We don't do that." Nurse Lili looked upset that they didn't check their patients' temperature as often in L 315.

"You were better with that. You were better with lots of things. Toilets too." Tony was trying his best to make her happy. "You sure it doesn't bother you that I'm taking my temperature while you visit?"

"Not at all," she said. "I'm just glad the mouse isn't making noise anymore. Apart from that, I don't have a worry in the world."

Helga had settled back down again.

Of course she hadn't been making noise on purpose. Probably Nurse Lili had bumped her leg against the box and frightened Helga. Tony didn't hold it against her. He knew from experience that Helga was a sensitive mouse. He felt pretty good right now too. Even though he wasn't wild about having to take his temperature.

Finally, Nurse Lili said, "Enough is enough," and took the thermometer away from him.

"You're fine," she said. "And you know what? I'm going to lie down here a while with you."

She pulled her sweater off over her head, then, turning her back to him, removed her stockings, or whatever it was they were.

She looks good in them, Tony thought. Maybe even more from behind than from in front. Her hair is so pretty. He glanced out the window and noticed a flock of geese heading west. "You see that?" he said. "Those are either swallows or partridges. You can tell by the way they fly. Can you see what they are?"

"No," said Nurse Lili. She lay down next to him.

Tony slid away a little. "Me neither," he said. "But you know what? When the Russians come, we won't be able to protect our animals for a while, but we can specialize in horses instead. What do you think?"

"Maybe," said Nurse Lili, shifting closer to him.

From the distance, from a great distance, came the sound of thundering cannons.

In closing, just a short note for those who were there.
Some of you may be upset that a lot of things
about your ghettos were different from the way
they are in Tony's ghetto. I realize that.
Blame it on my bad memory and my
incorrigible tendency toward literary
stylizing. Forgive me.

Yours truly, Pick.

LAUGHTER IN THE DARK

Jiří Robert Pick (1925–83), known to the initiated as J. R. Pick, satirist, was a mover and shaker of the legendary 1960s Prague theater scene, whose small stages served as centers of intellectual resistance in the political thaw that came in the wake of Stalin's death and the anti-Semitic purges throughout the East bloc.

At a time when Czech playhouses rang with the names Otomar Krejča, Alfréd Radok, and, from the younger generation, Václav Havel, Pick worked out of the Reduta experimental theater, writing shows with the famed Jiří Suchý and Ivan Vyskočil, in the genre they invented, known as the text-appeal. Based on the term "sex appeal," this was a form of literary cabaret, "appealing" to audiences through music and words to engage them on issues where debate in mainstream culture was lacking. Their innovativeness was typical of that era, when clubgoers in Prague were getting their first look at striptease, but in 1968, the prudish Czechoslovak Communists, who had previously sent their comrades to the gallows, called their overseers in Moscow to nip the country's newfound freedom in the bud.

Besides his work with Suchý and Vyskočil, Pick also engaged in public life as a journalist for *Literární noviny*, the leading outlet for voices of reform, as well as founding a theater company of his own, called Paravan, and in 1968–69, he ran the cabaret Au (for "Author's"), although it was shut down in the cultural freeze that followed the arrival of Warsaw Pact tanks in August 1968.

I was still in the crib in the days when theatergoers delighted to Pick's epigrams and satirical lyrics. When his books were removed from libraries and, along with hundreds of other writers, he was banned from publishing, I was just beginning to think for myself. But my father, Josef Topol, was a playwright who worked in the avant-garde Theater Beyond the Gate, so when the Soviets invaded and the Communists closed its doors, our flat became a magnet for banned figures, including Havel and actors Pavel Landovský and Jan Tříska, the young generation of rebels who eventually either emigrated or ended up in jail. Playwrights, actors, dramaturgs, technicians, stagehands—when everyone lost their jobs, the theater and literary scenes relocated to pubs and people's flats.

One of my clearest childhood memories is of a bearded gentleman with a strong slouch, glasses, and a ringing laugh. It may well have been Pick, who was known as not only one of the biggest jokesters, but also a tireless debater. As my younger brother Filip and I were chased off to bed, the discussions raged on, fueled by copious jugs of beer and bottles of wine. Czechs are known for their dark sense of humor, and in those days, under occupation by Russian tanks, it was especially black. Free art moved into the cellars and underground and stayed there, producing its bitter, darkly comic fruit until the eruption of revolutions in Eastern Europe decades later.

And what of Pick's *Society for the Prevention of Cruelty to Animals*? It came to me almost like a hallucination one morning in my youth when I was saved from the boredom of school by being home sick with the flu. Rummaging through my parents' bookshelves, I pulled out this slim volume. My first instinct, I admit, was to put it back. Like many children in those days, because of the propaganda we were subjected to in school, I had an aversion to anything having to do with World War II, and Pick throws you into the Terezín ghetto right from the start.[1] But after the first few pages, I was eager to keep reading, grinning my way through my fever, right to the end.

In Pick's story, Tony, the hero, who is roughly the same age as I was when I read the book, decides to set up a society for the prevention of cruelty to animals in the ghetto. But apart from fleas, lice, worms, and a Nazi officer's dog, there are no animals. Tony lives on the tuberculosis ward, surrounded by the quarrels of dying old men. Friends flash

1) Sometimes also referred to by its German name, Theresienstadt, Terezín was founded as a fortress town in the late eighteenth century. During World War II, the Nazi German regime used it as a transit camp for Czech Jews, before sending them on to other concentration, labor, and death camps (including Auschwitz), and as a ghetto and labor camp for German, Austrian, and Czech Jews. The town still exists, with part of it preserved as a memorial.

in and out, then disappear on a transport, along with young women so hungry they will trade sex for a dumpling, and in the background of it all, the Nazis' death machine grinds on inexorably. It's a genocidal comedy that is seriously no joke. There is no gallows humor here, provoking outbursts of laughter. An occasional splutter or faint smile, maybe; a shake of the head in disbelief that this singular survival manual, a work of traditional Jewish humor, was produced literally in sight of the execution grounds. And that it was written in prose. And published in 1969.

It was only much later I realized that Pick's measured, administratively tinged language was less inspired by classic Czech black humor, the boisterous gluttony of Hašek and Hrabal, than by that other famous Prague resident, Franz Kafka. And it was only much later that I submerged myself in Kafka, under the instruction and guidance of Pick.

One other thing came to mind as I read this unusual book, whose description, however chaste, of the Jewish bad boys' and girls' sexual games in a Catholic church, or its harsh portrayal of the tubercular old men, may still offend some to this day: I had heard those kinds of stories before, and heard them often. Right here in our very own kitchen. Stories told by Mr. Rappaport or Mr. Stach, stagehands from my dad's theater, about having the wrong size shoes on the death march and how so-and-so died because his shoes were too big. Or was it too little? And did he die, or did he survive? They laughed as they told the stories, and we laughed along, but it was no joke. They had been there in the camps.

After 1968, the humor of those who were banned by the Communists absorbed and intermingled with the humor of the former concentration camp prisoners whom they came to know as a result. No wonder the darkly comic tales of the Nazi camps merged in my little boy's head with the jokes about brutal and incompetent cops, or the stories of interrogations by the secret police. And as it turned out, seeing the world through a dark lens allowed me and my brother, and everyone else who grew up in that environment, to remain above it all, even when we were in dire straits—a tremendously helpful tool for coping with life in the art underground.

Pick and many others from the 1970s Czech underground—a community that poet Ivan Jirous dubbed the "merry ghetto" for its dignity, solidarity, and celebratory spirit—never stopped writing, even if their works were read "only" by a network of reliable friends.

Years later, I visited Terezín as a journalist, after the catastrophic floods of 1997 and 2002 caused the death of some fifty people and the overflowing Elbe damaged or destroyed much of the town. Natural disasters on this scale are a rare occurrence in the normally peaceful landscape of Bohemia. The Czech army, once garrisoned there, had long since left, taking with it many residents who had been dependent on the soldiers for their jobs, and the question hung in the air: What will become of the ghetto now? A place of pilgrimage and of suffering, a fortress town whose broken ramparts and evacuated inhabitants were turning it into a ghost town.

I walked among the ruins, perhaps unconsciously hoping to find the hospital building where Tony searched for an animal he could protect in this place of merciless death.

I met the locals, those few who had chosen to remain and try to save their town, in spite of the catastrophes that had befallen it. Some of their efforts were downright bizarre. A group of former soldiers who had set down roots there tried to pump it up as a tourist destination, reviving the old army shooting range and placing an ad on the internet urging visitors, "Come shoot in Terezín!" Their plan, fortunately, was met with outrage.

The government, too, sounded the alarm. Terezín, after all, only a daytrip away from Prague, was recognized as a commemorative site in every high school textbook. Ideas ranged from evacuating the rest of the inhabitants to vague plans of building a world university of Holocaust education. EU commissioners, officials from every state, descended on the town. I met young people from every corner of Europe, often third- or fourth-generation survivors of the Holocaust, rushing to the beleaguered town's aid. Many of them were clueless, wandering around the mass burial site with their drums and dreadlocks, evoking mainly disgust on the part of the locals. Yet they were there searching for something, trying to understand what had happened to their relatives so long ago and why it had happened. For them the bottom line was that this unfortunate town was at risk of being destroyed and this might be their last chance to save it.

It was these encounters that led me to write my pitch-black comedy *Chladnou zemí*, published in English as *The Devil's Workshop*. So perhaps it isn't too great a stretch to say Pick's humor lay at its roots: the belief that a good book is a culmination of anxiety, not an escape from it. Why is it so important to be able to joke about the greatest horrors? So that we don't choke to death on the blackness. Perhaps what I was after was that paralyzing flash of insight described by the Czech poète maudit Ladislav Klíma as the realization that "the horrible and the laughable are sisters."

It's also quite likely that the incredible cemetery scene in Pick's novella, where the gravediggers debate what's happening to the ghetto population, lies at the roots of my latest book. With the Allies advancing and trainloads of Jews shipping out of Terezín, what are the Germans doing with all of them? Shooting them? Hanging them? Either way, it's not economical. The most rational way to get rid of them would be drowning. A good-sized lake would easily hold a few million Jews, no trouble at all. The three men digging the grave bicker back and forth as Tony watches them bury his best friend.

In its use of a child's perspective to portray misery and dying in a matter-of-fact way, Pick's *Society for the Prevention of Cruelty to Animals* may be compared to "Miriam," a story set in Terezín by Ivan Klíma,[2] who was also imprisoned in the ghetto as a child. In Pick's book, an ailing boy is initiated

2) *My First Loves*, 1986, translated by Ewald Osers.

into adulthood through the affection, or love, of a young woman. What Klíma and many other authors depict as veiled and tragic, however, Pick describes with joy and humor. So, what about the animal that Tony so longs to protect? All his best friends are gone, most likely dead. And after all he's been through in the ghetto, Tony doesn't seem like such a little boy anymore. Sitting on his bed with a young woman, there's a box beneath the bed—and inside . . . could it be there's something alive in there? Maybe they will make it out after all.

I hope it won't sound like sacrilege—I even find it hard to write—but I believe Pick is looking for sparks of joy in what we know is hell. Perhaps that is the quality that Christians call grace, amazing grace.

Jáchym Topol
Prague, July 2017
Translated from the Czech by Alex Zucker

ABOUT MY BROTHER

After the Nazis banned Jewish children in Prague from attending school, in 1940, my brother and I spent a lot of time at home and had to depend on each other for company. I was happy to have my clever older brother around. Bobby (as my mother and I always called him), being six years older than me, was less than thrilled about it, but he often played with me, and talked with me about our favorite books by the German author Karl May. We had his complete works at home and knew by heart the names of all the characters and locations in his adventure novels set in the American Old West and other distant lands. Even then, Bobby was already writing constantly—mainly lyrical and satirical poems—and also translating poems from German, especially Goethe. He had no other audience, so he read it all to me, and every year for my birthday he would write me funny poems. It was a family tradition started by our grandmother, and Bobby excelled at it. I still have the one he wrote for me in Terezín, on my thirteenth birthday, based on one of our favorite games.

My family went to Terezín in the summer of 1943. (We had been assigned to a transport a year earlier, but I came down with scarlet fever, and since the Nazis were supposedly afraid of infections, our departure was postponed.) About a week after we arrived in the ghetto, Bobby came to the attic in house number Q 306, where my mother and I had been placed, and lay down next to me on the bed, saying he didn't feel well. In the evening, when he stood up to return to his quarters, he collapsed. He had polio. He was paralyzed, and we weren't sure if he would survive. (Eventually he recovered, but he walked with a strange gait for the rest of his life.)

As soon as Bobby felt better, he began to write again. I went every day to see him in the hospital, and sometimes delivered love poems from him to Věra Weislitzová, whom he had a crush on. Bobby was musically gifted as well, playing both the piano and the accordion. When they let him out of the hospital, he got a job playing accordion in the Terezín coffeehouse, but a short while after, he began coughing up blood and had to return to the hospital. This time it was tuberculosis, and he remained in the hospital until the end of the war.

When I first read my brother's Terezín book, published in Czech in 1969 as *Spolek pro ochranu zvířat*, I didn't know which parts were invented and which were actually based on his experience. "I think he went too far, making up that scene where Tony and his mother bet on which patient in the dying room is going to die next," I told my mother. But she replied: "He didn't make that up. When he was in the polio ward with all those little children, we used to make bets on it every day."

Bobby waited more than twenty years to write his book about Terezín. In the copy he gave me, he wrote: "To my little sister, who remembers it all differently." As usual, he was teasing me, but it's true, I think, that everyone remembers that terrible time a little differently.

Our father died in Auschwitz, and in 1948 my mother and I emigrated to Argentina. Bobby chose to stay in Prague. It was a hard good-bye. I missed my brother badly, but in spite of the enormous distance between us, we remained close. I went on reading and admiring his writing, and the conversation between us continued through our letters, with Bobby's poems, written in perfect rhyme, arriving in the mail to mark important moments in my life. At one point, when I was sick and bedridden for a long time, Bobby, who had more than his fair share of experience with illness, wrote me:

How often do I tell myself,
Better sick than in good health.
The ill man dreams of getting well,
The well man fears health gone to hell.

Now, whenever I think of my beloved brother and our endless conversations, I remember how much I always laughed.

Zuzana Justman is a documentary filmmaker living in New York.

TRANSLATOR'S ACKNOWLEDGMENTS

It has been fifteen years since Zuzana Justman first approached me about translating her brother's book *Spolek pro ochranu zvířat*, in 2002.

My thanks go to Jáchym Topol, who wrote the afterword to this volume, but also, together with Viktor Stoilov, showed me around Terezín in 2011, while I was working on *The Devil's Workshop,* my translation of his novel *Chladnou zemí,* part of which is set in modern-day Terezín. That experience was important to me on this project.

First and foremost, though, I wish to thank Zuzana herself, for trusting me to bring into English a book so close to her heart. I enjoyed every one of the conversations we had about the translation, and consider myself fortunate to know a person of her caliber.

Alex Zucker, Brooklyn, NY November 2017

ABOUT THE TRANSLATOR

Alex Zucker (b. 1964) has translated novels by Jáchym Topol, Petra Hůlová, Patrik Ouředník, Heda Margolius Kovály, Tomáš Zmeškal, and Magdaléna Platzová. He is winner of an English PEN Award for Writing in Translation, an NEA Literary Fellowship, and the ALTA National Translation Award. In addition to translating, he has worked in journalism and human rights. His most recent translations are *Three Plastic Rooms*, by Petra Hůlová, and *Angel Station*, by Jáchym Topol. His last translation for Karolinum Press was *Midway Upon the Journey of Our Life*, by Josef Jedlička.